Table 52 - A Second Collection of Short Stories

Table 52 Writers et al.

To Nomie
with love
Ruth

Published by Table 52 Writers, 2022

These stories are works of fiction. Similarities to real people. Places, or events are entirely coincidental.

TABLE 52 - A SECOND COLLECTION OF SHORT STORIES

First edition July 20th, 2022

Written by Table 52 Writers et al.

Foreword

Nine writers. Fifteen stories. Nine voices. No – more: every good story contains not just the voice of the writer but those of their characters. In these pages there are dozens, each of them calling out for your attention. They sound from across the globe and across time: Aegean, Thailand, London, 1930s Iraq, 1960s America. This is not surprising. The Table 52 Writers, although first meeting in my writing class at Richmond Adult Community College, have roots in Turkey, Paris and across the UK. Each of their tales is a snapshot of what it is like to live in Human City.

This is the second Table 52 anthology. Their first showcased a bunch of vivid, well-crafted stories. In this they have dug deeper into their subject matter and characters and found some very rich seams. The tone is as varied as the settings. Comedy is well represented: Trevor Aston's "Heatwave" is a witty alternative history set in the hardboiled world of the American music business, Sarah Savage's "Bilk" is a caustic satire on Thai brides, Joe de Souza writes Pythonesque flights of fancy and Flavie Salaun's "A Cat in the Dark" is a delicious modern comedy of manners. Deborah Reeves gives us three acute glimpses of modern unease. Frank Offer's "The Beach" is a haunting tale of middle-aged longing while Karen Ali's "Waiting for the King" captures the fervour of boyhood hopes. An encounter in a hospital support group leads to a touching friendship in Celia Grey's "The Phone Call". The protagonist in

Sinem Erenturk's atmospheric "Silence of Olive Trees" finds that even in an idyllic coastal resort it's hard to dissipate the memories of an oppressive marriage.
This collection is a small masterpiece of collaboration. Each story belongs to its writer – have no fear of that – but it grew out of weekly meetings held by the group in which they share dreams, ideas, and critiques, as well as the large and the tiny editorial choices. Writing is a hard and lonely road with as many potholes as heights. More writers should co-operate like this.
Read this book at one sitting or savour each story over time. I hope you enjoy them as much as I have.

Tony Kirwood, writer and teacher

Creative writing is important because it helps us understand ourselves and others and helps to improve readers' wellbeing. I am therefore delighted to see RHACC writers' creative journey extending beyond the classroom and have enjoyed escaping into the characterful works in the collection, each with its own distinctive voice.

Gabrielle Flint, Principal, Richmond & Hillcroft

Adult Community College

Contents

Blood Oranges, Guavas and Believing in Fairies

By Deborah Reeves

Every week Mary and her sister went to the shop on the top road to get the Sunday papers. Their dad said they could keep the change. It was always the same, sixpence each, enough to buy a comic or some sweets.

There were grass verges and bushes on one side of the lane and fields on the other. Mary was looking for fairies. The golden ones were best. They were the ones who put drops of water on cobwebs and along the edges of leaves. Sometimes she caught a glimpse from the corner of her eye, flickers of gold, but they disappeared as soon as she turned. They were quick. Their Uncle Ted worked in the shop so they were allowed to cut through the alley to the back. It was cool and dark and there were sacks of knobbly potatoes. We're very special, Mary thought. No one else can come in. She sat on a sack and breathed in the earthy smell.

'Do fairies come in here?' she asked her sister. Her sister said she doubted it and 'Get off that sack.'

It was light and bright inside the shop. Uncle Ted was behind the counter in his white overalls. Behind him were huge jars sparkling with sweets: pear drops, sherbet lemons, aniseed balls, gobstoppers, and in front, in thin cardboard boxes, two-a-penny chews, black jacks, fruit salads, fizzers and sherbet dip dabs, love hearts, liquorice sticks and bubble gum. Mary watched as Uncle Ted handed her sister the papers.

'Hurry up and pick your sweets,' her sister said. Mary knew her sister wanted to buy a comic, Jackie, and that she wasn't allowed to. It was something to do with boys and kissing. Her mother and sister talked about things like that a lot and Mary would watch them, not able to join in.

'What'll you be having then?' Uncle Ted said.

Mary pointed to the ones she wanted and Uncle Ted dropped them in a white paper bag and gave her two extras.

As they walked back, her sister said, 'Have you seen any of these fairies then?'

'They won't let me see them,' Mary bit her lip.

'Why don't you leave them some presents. Then they might let you.'

'I left them pencil sharpenings for dresses but they didn't take them.'

'Oh, but it has to be something really special,' her sister said, taking Mary's hand. 'Something they'd really like. Something delicious.' And so every week Mary left her sweets out for the fairies and it was several weeks before she realised that she'd been tricked. Her sister was good at tricking.

Once her sister told Mary that blood oranges were red from the blood of Spanish men buried beneath the trees. Mary could imagine the trees black against a gold sunset, white roots wrapped around the Spanish men's bodies, drawing up their blood. She didn't want to eat them any more but her mother would still offer them to her and laugh.

Her mother and sister often ganged up on her. They both

loved tinned guavas. Slimy, gritty, pink tomatoes. Mary hated them.

'Oh, we forgot you don't like them,' they said and made slurping noises as they ate, showing their delight, giving her sideways glances. She felt her lip tremble but held her face firm.

One time her mother incited Mary's sister to drag Mary up the stairs by her hair and said, 'Let's not talk to her. Pretend she isn't there.'

That day Mary found that she could float high above them, surrounded by flickers of gold. She could slit her eyes and peer at them as if from a tower.

'Look at her. Away with the fairies,' they laughed, but they couldn't reach her.

Mary smiled to herself. She knew she had the best trick of all.

***

Bob Saved the Queen

By Joe De Souza

Bob believed he had already foiled a terrorist threat at Heathrow airport in the late seventies. He reckoned he had diffused a bomb while working there as an electrician. He is awaiting his knighthood.

During his stint at the airport, Bob had become aware of a ticking noise coming from a child's rucksack. When he had the chance, he rifled through the unattended bag and removed the device. Although it had a Micky Mouse cover on it, he wasn't to be deterred.

'That's not going to fool me,' he said and with determination he moved to a safe distance from the crowds, and painstakingly removed the battery, sweat dripping from his brow.

When Bob had told his old friend Rodney, he was almost star struck.

Of course, they both knew that his real recognition was going to be from the Queen herself, in the form of a knighthood.

Rodney was a simple man and a good friend of Bob's. He

would often come over for tea first thing in the morning. They would tell each other stories about their earlier lives; Bob having left home early to join the merchant navy, while Rodney laid claim to having served in the Royal Navy. Bob didn't believe him, but he never said.

The next morning, Rodney arrived at Bob's as usual. But Bob had visions, bigger than chats over tea. He'd had a premonition in the form of a dream: the Queen was in danger. It was time for action and yet again, Bob was ready.

'Rodney,' Bob said, 'lend us a fiver. I'm off to save the Queen.' Rodney didn't hesitate and Bob was gone in a flash.

The journey was insubstantial compared to the vital message he needed to pass on. Once there, he marched up to a soldier and spoke.

'I'd like to speak to the adjutant.'

The adjutant duly arrived, responding quickly enough to his message Bob felt and then Bob spoke out in a commanding voice.

'I have some very important news to pass on to the Queen.'

'Yes, of course. Can I have your name sir?'

'The name is Bob—but let's move on to more urgent matters.'

Bob now feeling a very real sense of importance and was also impatient due to the urgency.

'Buckingham Palace and the whole of London are in imminent danger. There is a risk of a bomb.'

'Thank you, Bob,' said the adjutant. 'You are a fine man; I shall pass the message on.'

Bob, pleased to have got some authoritative recognition, moved on.

Later, Rodney had been waiting and asked him what happened next.

'She was out the side gate of Buckingham Palace, onto her souped-up gold-plated Yamaha 50cc moped, and over

Chertsey Bridge and down the Staines Road before the emergency services could keep up with her.'

'Crikey,' said Rodney. 'Did she get a chance to put her crash helmet on?'

'Are you joking? We're talking about the Queen here. Nothing but the best and that includes her crown!'

Finally, she arrived at Windsor Castle and into relative safety, where Bob was awaiting her arrival.

'She must have been very grateful. What did she say?' Rodney asked.

'Bob, I don't know how you do it.'

'I expect she was in a state of shock when she arrived. Did she have a roll-up and a stiff drink?'

Bob puffed out his chest indignantly and replied, 'The Queen doesn't smoke roll-ups. She's on twenty Lambert and Butler a day.'

'Bob, you're a great man.'

'Thank you,' he replied.

***

Heatwave

By Trevor Aston

The doorbell chimes. The note of F, followed after four seconds by C, with a sustain as long as your arm. Gorgeous. I had it made from a couple of tubular bells I found in the rubble of a bombed-out music school somewhere in Berlin, 1945.

I open my front door. I'm expecting a delivery, but instead I find my friend Kenny.

'You? What are you doing here at this time?'

'I've got a lyric.' He holds up a piece of paper as he says it, as if he's serving me with a court order. He's popping with excitement. Kenny and me write songs. He does the squiggles, I do the dots.

'It's called Heatwave.' He walks in and I shut the door.

'So, you've driven across New York through a blizzard? When the forecast says it isn't going over minus five degrees? With a lyric called Heatwave? Dearest Kenny, what are you on?'

'Hey, I can't help it when the muse takes me. It needs a tune, my English friend.'

'Ok. But how, why? I mean, it is freezing out there.'

'I know it's freezing, remember I just came in from out there?' Kenny drops his coat on the floor. This annoys me.

'Don't just drop your coat on the floor. A nice Astrakhan like that deserves more respect.' He's gone straight to the kitchen.

'In fact, Kenny, I can't help feeling that I deserve more respect. Make yourself at home, why don't you?'

'We go back too far to be propping up propriety. Especially when there's salami to be piled.' That is Kenny's euphemism for writing music. I don't understand it either. 'Do you want a coffee too?'

'Why, Kenny, that would be awfully kind of you.' It's my home and yet he is offering me coffee.

'So, you know I've got to do a lyric for a movie, pronto?' Work, and therefore filthy lucre, seem to gravitate towards Kenny, which has been great for me too. We have a different attitude to money. I never had much, but now I do, I like it. And I like to spend it. Kenny's always had it.

'How could I forget, my so-called partner is writing a song without me.' Don't get me wrong. I'm not jealous, he's a lyrical wizard.

'What can I say, the movie's already scored. Anyway, I only got it because a certain someone is in jail after a certain incident with a certain young lady.'

'Who was it?'

'The girl? I don't know.'

'No, who's writing the score?'

'I can't tell you.'

'Ok. Well, I expect I'll find out when the credits roll.'

'Look, I don't want to say because it won't make you happy.'

At this point, Kenny starts grinding coffee. And keeps on grinding.

‘Kenny, I think you’ve ground enough,’ I shout at him. ‘There’s only so much coffee in Brazil.’ He takes his finger off the button and a deep draw of the aroma.

‘So, this isn’t the song you’re writing for the film?’ I say, waving the manuscript he just gave me.

‘No, that I haven’t written that yet. It can wait.’

‘Didn’t you just tell me the film people needed it quickly? Pronto, you said?’

‘Only semi-pronto, though it might end up super-pronto. But that song in your hand is a gift from Euterpe.’

‘Who?’ He ignores my question. His eyes are wide, I think he’s been up all night.

‘I’ve been up all night, but when you got the muse, you’ve got to make use.’ That’s ‘use’ pronounced to rhyme with ‘muse’ in case you missed it. Sometimes, Kenny just talks in song lyrics.

‘And you got the muse landing on you like the snow on Central Park.’ I observe.

‘You’re right. Picture it, I’m in my study looking at big, fluffy, white flakes swirling around the trees and I’m chilled through to the marrow.’

‘I sympathise. Your study's only good for spring and the autumn. Summer’s too hot and winter’s too cold.’

‘You’re right again, but I was trying to come up with something for the movie and they need a summery song. So, I say to myself, “Kenny, think warm.” I picture beaches, bikinis, blue skies, Bellinis in Harry’s bar. It’s gonna be a heatwave.’

‘Pretty much your first line, Kenny.’

‘Well, it’s the best place to start.’

‘And why can’t they have this for the film?’

‘It doesn’t fit. Read it, but sit at your piano. I don’t want to miss any musical stirrings.’ It takes little encouragement for me to perch on a piano stool, and it’s best to ride the rollercoaster of Kenny's enthusiasm. One minute he's saying a lyric is the best thing since pitted prunes, the next it's like he's gulping sour milk. This lyric is neither of those.

While I'm reading, Kenny has been appraising my apartment. 'This place is a mess, what my scotch aunt would call a "midden". Did you fire your help?'

It comes back to me just where I was when Kenny tolled the doorbell - upstairs with the help. Well, I needed a little help and it turned out she likes an English accent. Kenny goes back to making himself a coffee. He seems to have forgotten about my cup. I read his lyric.

Beaches, bikinis, blue skies, Bellinis, it's a scorcher, shimmering the sand.

A blazing eye, hanging in the sky, fissuring the land, we're all gonna fry.

That's just the introduction. It's all I can give you here as apparently there's a licensing issue. So I can't quote any more from the song.

'Kenny, you write your lines too long.'

'No, I don't. The lines are the length they need to be. There's the beginning, there's the end. I write just enough words to fill the gap.' You can almost hear the sound of heels being dug in.

'They don't need to be that long.' Now it's my turn to be stubborn. 'You just have to take the full stop and move it nearer the beginning.'

'Short lines, long lines, just go put some dots on those five lines.' He's pointing to a piece of manuscript. 'Go finger the black and whites.'

Now at this point the help walks in wearing my towelling robe. It's just a shortie, my robe. As it happens, so is the help. But it's obvious that under the robe she's as raw as the weather. Kenny looks at me as if I'm Salieri claiming the authorship of Eine Kleine.

'I see it wasn't the keyboard you were planning on fingering,' he says.

'What can I say? She works hard, she gets hot.' I am a little embarrassed.

'Oh, I believe you.' says Kenny.

With my thanks, my best smile and $20 for a cab, I send the help on her way. I also promise to do some cleaning before she comes back. Then, Kenny and I get down to piling salami on Heatwave. An hour and a quarter later, honestly, that's all it was. An hour and a quarter later, we've written ourselves a nice little ditty. You know what, there's more to Kenny's lyric than I thought. At least it's inspired a charming melody for Heatwave.

'That's not bad my friend,' says Kenny.

'I don't often agree with you, Kenny, but on this occasion, I think I do.'

'I'm honoured,' he says regally.

'I am honoured,' I say.

'I'm honoured by you honouring me,' he says.

'Maybe we can both be honoured?' I suggest.

'I've almost forgotten why we're honouring ourselves.' Kenny says.

'Because, old chap, the song we've just written is the cat's pyjamas.'

'You're right. In fact my friend, I'd go so far as to say it's the ant's pants.'

'As your scotch aunt would say?'

'Yep,' Kenny confirms, putting on his Astrakhan.

'I'd love to meet her.' I don't mean it, Scots never like me.

'She's dead.'

'Oh, I'm sorry Kenny. Well, maybe in the next life.'

'Only if you go to hell.'

I open the door for him.

'Bye, Kenny.'

'Toodle pip, my English friend.' And he's gone.

*

The next day, Kenny's on the phone convincing me we should celebrate with lunch. I'm happy to stay in my apartment. Today is just as cold as yesterday, but Kenny is saying he'll pay. Don't get me wrong. I love Kenny like he's my brother, but the man is a skinflint, always last to the bar. So, when Kenny offers to buy lunch it's like opening the door and finding a leprechaun holding a four-leaf clover. I'm not going to turn him down. But I do have to convince him not to drive.

'I'll call a cab, Kenny.'

'I'm taking my car.'

He's got a dark red, 1958 Thunderbird rag-top. Very nice.

'Leave the car, we can take a cab. Let's open a bottle of fizz and drink a toast to Heatwave.'

'I'm taking my car.'

He's a terrible driver.

'You think I'm a terrible driver.'

'Kenny, the roads are covered with snow and ice. You do so many things well, but I don't think driving is one of them.'

*

Well, we've arrived and Kenny is handing his keys to the valet. It was a compromise. I drove as far as Sixth Avenue, then we swapped so Kenny could drive up Fifth to the Plaza. It's a little early for me to be celebrating, but after that drive I could do with a relaxant. The Oak Bar is almost empty, just a guy with his back to us. He's wearing a fedora hat. Why do people keep their hat on once they've come indoors? I see the bartender measuring out Jack Daniels, just two fingers, very carefully so the man in the fedora hat can see. Then he counts four rocks of ice and pours the JD over them. To be frank, that drink and that fedora could only be one man, and that would be Frank.

'Don't try to be his friend by mixing that heavy,' I say to the bartender, loud enough for the fedora hat to hear.

The head under the fedora turns round to see who's quoting him, clocks it's me and smiles. We've written for Frank before, so I know he likes his Jack Daniels done his way, exactly his way, or woe betide the barman.

Kenny is in there faster than JD bites the back of your throat. 'JD on the rocks, they go together like love and marriage, don't you think Frank?' he says.

Frank motions us to sit, then to the bartender to make two more.

'Great to see you, Frank,' I say.

'So what are you guys doing here at this ungodly hour?' The crooner asks.

'Celebrating, Mr Success.' Kenny's over excited, slipping in Frank's songs.

'You guys been piling the salami?' Frank asks, almost knocking me of my stool with surprise that he too knows this odd idiom.

'We have, and we've got high hopes.' See what Kenny did there?

'Well, since I'm buying the drinks, can I get a little preview?' Frank's rinsing his rocks in a little more JD.

'You can hear it, Frank,' I tell him, 'but my friend and I might not do it justice.'

'I have to sing it my way, Frank.' I have a strong suspicion that Kenny's been sitting there waiting for a chance to slip that in.

'Come on, you guys. You know me and half-baked from you two is better than a panettone from Tin Pan Alley.' You see why Frank doesn't write his own songs.

We're still the only customers in the piano bar. I play while Kenny sings. One thing I will say for the Plaza, they keep the Bush and Gerts in tune. It is a pity they can't do the same for

Kenny. Have you heard Kenny sing? A fingernail scraped along a blackboard has more music, but of course Frank's got an ear for a song. He hears it through, then asks to hear it again.

'That, boys, is the best song I've heard in a long time.' Kenny and I wait for the punchline. 'I mean it, boys. I want to record it.'

Obviously, you don't want to turn down Frank.

'I'm gonna call Joey, he'll fix it.' You don't turn down Joey either.

'Don't worry, boys,' Frank adds, maybe sensing what we're thinking. That sometimes Joey's 'fix' isn't so good for everybody else. But we smile for Frank. It's best to.

*

Well, there's a little bit of to-ing and fro-ing with our publisher, but in the end, Joey gives us a particularly good deal. Which is particularly good news for me, since my accountant says he can't hold off the IRS any longer. They're looking at everything, right back to the first wordy-warble Kenny and I bulldozed into the hit parade. It was The Shadows Under Your Eyes. You might know it. The IRS doesn't believe I made nothing the year we wrote it. I find it hard to believe too. But there was Kenny fresh from college and me escaping Her Majesty's invitation to carry a Lee Enfield. While you could say we were both a little dewy-eyed in business, no one could say it of the publisher. Never mind, Kenny always reminds me, we've written a few more hits since then.

*

'Hey kid, what was it I told you about success breeding success?' Kenny's on the phone. 'I just got out of a meeting with Stanley.' I don't who he means.

'Which Stanley? Don't just say Stanley like I should know which Stanley you're talking about, or I must be a just-off-the-boat who doesn't know his Stanley from his elbow.'

'The Stanley with the movie that's breaking box office records?'

I think for a moment. 'Oh, that Stanley.'

'Yes, that Stanley, of course that Stanley. The Stanley who wants Heatwave for the soundtrack of his next box office record-breaking movie.'

'With Frank singing?' I ask.

'With Sammy singing it,' Kenny says, enjoying my surprise.

'No, and Frank's ok with that?'

'Maybe Stanley's people spoke to Frank's people and Frank's people spoke to Sammy's people. And Sammy's people just like the song. How the fuck should I know?'

You don't often hear Kenny swear.

'Kenny, I'll tell you what I know. I know I've got the IRS on my back like a cowboy at the rodeo and I'd be really happy if Frank sings Heatwave on his new album and Sammy sings it in Stanley's new movie.'

*

It was all going to happen, poised, primed, cocked. But bamma-bamma-bing, Motown gets in first with its own hit called Heat Wave and it's number one on the Billboard chart. But don't get confused, it is not the song called Heatwave that Kenny and I wrote. It is Heat Wave. Do you know it? It's going to be a classic. No, it is a classic.

'Frank wants me to change the title from Heatwave.' Kenny rings me when he hears the news. 'Maybe change everything, it's the tune he really likes.'

'So, let's do it.' I really don't want to lose this. 'It's got to be worth it, we won't always have Frank's ear.'

'Na, it's a wretched chorus and the verses are lousy.' Kenny's crossed over from the sunny side of the street.

'So write something better, Kenny.'

'So you think it's chickenshit too?'

'I didn't say that.'

'With some work, perhaps, I can move it from chickenshit to crappy.'

'Or maybe to exceptional?'

'Mediocre would be my best hope.'

'You're sounding a little down Kenny.'

'Down? If I climb a thousand stairs, I'll only just be getting to down.'

'Come on, Kenny, think of the money.' I admit I'm getting desperate.

'I don't need the money.'

'Well, I do.'

It's the nature of heatwaves that they don't last. That was the last time Kenny and I spoke.

*

Until today.

'So, wadyagonnado?' Kenny asks, shrugging. We're in a bar downtown, drinking cocktails.

'You didn't have to do that, Kenny.' He's signed over the rights to our last number so I can give something to the IRS. He just shrugs.

'Well, I'm grateful to you.' I say.

'I am also grateful to you, my English friend.'

'I think I have more to be grateful for.'

'My gratitude is immeasurable.' I can see he won't give in.

'Kenny, let's agree we're both grateful.'

'Ok. So, wadyagonnado?'

'Que sera sera, Kenny.'

'Que sera sera. You are right my friend, what will be, will be.'

'Que sera sera,' I repeat, a bit more singsong.

'Wait a minute, wait a minute.' Kenny sits up, suddenly excited. 'I think I've got another idea for a song.'

'I hate to disappoint you Kenny, but I think it's been done.'

***

The Phone Call

By Celia Gray

The hospital meeting for the breast cancer support group was about to begin. This seminar was conceived for the most vulnerable among the patients on the way to recovery, after having undergone operations and treatments. Next to me was Maggie, tall, well-groomed in her early sixties, mousy brown hair, a blouse, a skirt and a quiet voice. Her look was gentle and discerning. We were immediately drawn to each other.

The sun was streaming in through the large windows and I could see the branches of the giant trees swaying in the breeze. They looked lush and green, soothing. We were seated at a long table in this large space where the buzz of conversation became oppressive. Should I have agreed to these meetings? How could this possibly help the cancer?

The group leader dealt with the introductions and gave out paper, brushes and paints. Later I learned that the colours and design you chose pointed to your frame of mind. My painting consisted of pitch-black contours over the stark white sheet. That done, I looked around me and saw an exodus towards the tea break. Putting down brush and paints

I stared at the floor.

Someone said, 'Would you like some tea?' It was the quiet voice.

Surprised, I said, 'Don't know where to go. I expect, now there'll be a long queue.'

'Never mind that, come with me.'

On the way we talked while getting our buns, asked about the buses and where we lived. It all seemed so natural. I had to admit that was not what I expected. This person, Maggie, had extended a helping hand, the only one from the group to do so. This small gesture broke the spiral of anxiety and isolation within me, so that when paper and paint brushes came round a second time, my picture was punctuated with bright colours: a considerable mood change. The leader was so pleased that she mentioned this fact to the group.

At the end of the session, I said to Maggie, 'What do you do? Sorry to ask.'

'I have a medical background, research. You?'

'Literary, taught several languages, and divorced. Recently that is.'

'Never been married, me.'

We hurried out.

'Till next time,' Maggie said.

'Look forward to it.'

As I waited for the bus I thought about Maggie. With her knowledge of medicine she would be aware of every terrible outcome during the long process of recovery. I was protected from that fate by total ignorance. Come to think of it, I was quite taken aback as to how much I talked about myself. After all she was a total stranger, not like me at all. What devil possessed me to mention the divorce?

The following month, lighter of step, I approached the hospital and looked for Maggie; a kind of beacon in the midst of the sea of faces. She was sitting next to a middle-aged blonde, who fidgeted as she talked about being a single mother with children and one of them enlisted in a conflict zone. The leader spoke in low tones as she came round to squeeze her hand.

'How can anyone remain sane in such a mess?' I said.

'She will take it step by step. She'll manage,' Maggie answered.

As we got the tea, I asked about meeting later on.

'Yes, shortly after the group, on the premises,' she replied.

It was less crowded now as people went home for dinner. We found a table in a quiet corner by the window, the furthest away from the ever-present queue for tea and sandwiches. Both of us faced the window in order to escape the listless expressions of the patients and the forced smiles of the visitors. An enveloping aroma of ground coffee rose to our nostrils. It took me back to a happier place, to my parents drinking coffee on the veranda warmed by the winter sun.

'The divorce?' Maggie asked.

Jolted back to the moment, I bit my lip. 'The divorce, yes; loss, separation and upheaval. Nothing the same, ever again. I spent years being a wife and mother and now I am no longer a wife and motherhood has shrunk with the children marrying and leaving home. An empty cottage in a new neighbourhood where I know no one, and this illness. Who am I and what will I do all day? Set adrift, adrift . . . '

'Anything constant, anything that stayed the same?' she asked.

'Yes, my two cats remain, they are a source of great comfort. The other was my teaching but by then, I had retired. Do you have any pets?'

Maggie looked pensive and said she had none. Her mother didn't like them.

'A shame!'

'Live round here?' Maggie continued.

'Yes. And you?'

'Local now. Worked in Wales.'

'Interesting. Never been.'

'You know, beautiful country, people warm and friendly. That helped me because of my shyness. People came over to you which made it easier to connect. Back here for the treatment. Thinking of retirement, semi-retired now. '

'Family, did you see them?' I asked.

'No. Mother was the reason for going away,' she said. 'Father a fair man, civil engineer, often at work. There was me and an older brother. Ordered house. Church on Sundays.'

'Sounds idyllic.'

'It could have been. And there was a beautiful puppy called Trouble.'

I thought she said no pets. I waited. At last I said, 'Can you tell me about Trouble?'

Maggie gave a deep sigh. 'When I was seven, our neighbour's dog had a litter and I loved one puppy called Trouble. When the neighbour asked me if I wanted him, I said there was nothing in the whole world I wanted more. But Mother was against it. She said she would speak to Father.

'The next day I hurried home only to be intercepted by my brother. He nudged me saying, "Trouble? Why not a cat?" And continued with his remarks throughout the afternoon. Dinner was unbearable. Mother cleared the table and came to sit beside me saying that a dog was a distraction from my studies. She paused for a moment and added, "Now, toodeleedo, homework and bed."

'I sprang up, telling Mother that I liked the dog and wanted it. Of course, I did not intend to answer her. Right away, she came back at me as to how I thought she was touched to even consider a dog. I looked at Father, silently pleading for help. Father met my gaze for a fraction of a second and looked away. I knew then that all was lost. I repeated that I would do anything, anything if she agreed. Mother simply told me to get on with my homework.'

My heart went out to this little girl and her puppy.

'That was cruel,' I said.

Maggie nodded and added, 'Not only me, Dad . . .'

'Your father as well?'

'When I was around ten years old we were invited to our neighbour for tea. Our hostess had left the swatches for her new carpet on the mantelpiece. Mother examined the lush, deep pile and noted the colour and type. "Better than ours," she muttered softly to herself. That evening she was at the door to greet Father as he removed his hat and coat. She said hello and offered him a drink after a hard day. As Father took a sip of his whisky he looked round him as if he expected something. Mother came to sit beside him and asked about a particularly difficult client.

'In due course, the swatches were produced and displayed with loving care. Father looked like a caged animal, saying that they had already talked about it. Mother invited him to look at the quality, but he still said that funds were not available. Mother then suggested minor adjustments, longer hours, club membership . . . When he protested that he already worked harder than anyone he knew, she casually mentioned Scotland. I could picture the scene unfold in front of my eyes as he began. "Surely you don't mean that. My mother looks forward to our visits."

"Darling, of course we'll see your mother in Scotland, just not as often. It's only temporary."

'Father got up to answer the door and came back, saying that he thought someone was there.

"I want this, darling. Very much," Mother continued.

'Detecting the burning smell of the roast Father got up a second time. The conversation ended but not before Mother had secured his consent for an appointment with the store on

Saturday morning. That evening Father was off his food, made his excuses and retired early to bed.'

I looked away from the pain gathering on Maggie's face and took her hand. *A child witnessing such a scene and the untold damage!* I said, 'How old were you, ten?

'Yes.'

'You knew already how things were.'

'Yes.'

'Look at the time, it is late,' I said.

'Let's go.'

Outside, clouds were forming, rain threatened while the wind tore through the branches of the tall trees. We said our goodbyes, gathered our belongings and like two teenage girls, rushed to the buses to get home.

*

At the hospital for the third session, only two more left. Maggie came in late and sat at the far end of the table. I noticed that she was walking in a strange way. She seemed to put hardly any pressure on the left leg and tried to drag it when no one was looking. I made a mental note to get the tea for us.

At the break we settled down.

Maggie began, 'Are you alright?'

'Yes, I think so. You?'

'Overall, yes. A slight concern about my leg.'

'Oh?'

'The left. I ordered further tests today.'

'As a precaution, of course,' I said, my chest constricting a little.

'Of course.'

At the end of the session we bought our drinks and hurried to find a table. Maggie was now looking right at me.

She began, 'I have settled my affairs.'

I looked at her, frozen. Oh God, I thought, not now, not

ever. 'Me too,' I said at last. 'A simple will, everything to be divided in half for each of my two children.'

'I have no issue,' she continued. 'I had to think long and hard . . . my two favourite nephews, for a house, a flat, what they need.'

'That is good.' I was nearly choking, hoped she hadn't noticed. My eyes stayed on the trees beyond.

Conversation deserted us. The silence became heavy but still neither spoke. Maggie's face clouded over. She remained perfectly still.

'Shall we go?' she said. 'We can talk at length next time.'

*

As we assembled for the fourth session the tension began to rise: for some of us, the path cleared while for others health complications surfaced. Maggie was seated at the far end of the table. I fidgeted with my scarf and wondered about her test results. Later, we talked over dry, oversweet buns.

'The tests?' I asked.

'Next week,' she replied calmly.

Maggie seemed distant and remained immobile for a few minutes. 'You know,' she said, 'The last time we talked . . . I remembered . . . I somehow need to say . . . to tell you—'

'Did anything change?' I ventured.

'No. Matters got progressively worse. At eleven, Lucy, me and two other classmates were to make a foursome in our sleeping bags and a tent under the direction of the school authorities. On that occasion, I was forbidden on health grounds. In similar circumstances my brother went, but then he was a boy. Soon enough, Lucy became the only friend I was occasionally allowed to see. At fourteen, make-up and mini-skirts were banned and when I objected, going out was added to the list.'

'Terrible, terrible . . .' I murmured.

'And then there was cheeky, toothless Tommy: "Toothless"

was what his mates called him as a joke. Mother had certainly not counted on him. Tommy was part of the football team. A boy with ginger hair, a wide smile and drainpipe jeans, who out of the blue, began to take an interest in me. Being shy I ignored him. He persevered. He started walking me halfway home. I liked him; he helped me with physics. One day he asked if we could have extra time on Wednesdays When I said I couldn't that week, he asked about the next. I knew better than to talk to Mother. I asked Lucy to say I was with her. She became quiet and refused. Finally, she agreed, just for a few meetings.

'Just before the summer holidays, my brother saw us; must have seen us sitting in McDonald's with a drink and a portion of fries. We were oblivious to the crowds of youngsters milling about, the constant noise, the shouts of the food orders and the smell of greasy fried food. We had each other. I went home but this time to face a storm. Mother was already in my room opening all my drawers and reading everything she could find. The screaming and interrogation. My brother smirked as he passed me in the corridor. It was him. He must have told them.

'The following day I was grounded. That afternoon we were bundled in the car on our way to Dorset for a week's holiday by the sea. And then, I spent the summer with my aunt in Scotland which proved to be even worse than home. Upon my return in September Lucy explained that Tommy's family had moved away. Quietly, she handed me a sealed envelope. I waited until I was locked in my bedroom, in complete privacy, before reading the letter:

Dear Maggie

You will have heard a lot of rumours: this is the truth.

I started talking to you as a dare from the boys who said I would fail. At first it was that, but then we became friends. I like you very much. I am sorry that your family won't let me see you. That just upsets me so much. I imagine it was not much better for you.

Love, Tommy

'I treasured that note for many years. The girls taunted me without mercy because they knew about the bet. I felt vindicated at last. He did care, he said so.'

Maggie stopped. Her hands were shaking. I took them into mine.

'Fourteen and your first love, tender and overwhelming. Should have been handled with sensitivity.'

'Impossible for Mother; it escaped her control.'

'That is awful. And your father?'

'You know. Could not go against her.'

'So sorry,' I explained. 'I don't know how this feels; I was much loved as a child, indulged even. But then I suppose the marriage ended, not loved, perhaps not loved enough . . . ' I let go of her hands. Now I was talking aimlessly again, 'I suppose that was what my friend meant, about wounds from the past; they cannot be removed, but the pain dulls.'

Maggie drank her tea, settled back in her chair and looked through the window. We gathered our belongings and headed to the buses in total silence. I noticed that Maggie's walking had deteriorated further. At any rate, to worry now is hardly productive. If you think about it, that will make it happen, just don't think about it, don't think about it. We'll know for certain next time with the results.

*

Two days prior to the last seminar, I had a health check and was given the all clear, for the time being. I was overjoyed, upbeat and energetic. Somehow that functioned like a mist that masked uncomfortable truths. I assumed that my friends would also be well. At the meeting, Maggie was quiet. Right away, I blurted out my question about the tests. She replied that some results were not clear cut and the tests had to be repeated.

'Oh, we have to wait yet again!' I mumbled. Maggie ignored the remark.

As the seminar drew to a close we instinctively looked at each other, long and hard as if to fix the images in our minds, and forever. We had travelled the long road together and shared intimate details of our lives with virtual strangers. Most of us were in tears. Maggie and I agreed to continue the hospital coffees. She looked calm and in total control. Though, I couldn't help wondering, wondering . . .

'Portugal, that one sticks in my mind,' Maggie began out of the blue.

'At seventeen, Mother persuaded us to accompany her to Portugal to see her friends. Forever the expectant optimist, I accepted. She chose a good hotel and we saw the friends for outings. One day we were having drinks on the veranda when their children, teenagers then, invited me and my brother to a disco. The smile faded from Mother's lips. She promptly took me inside and blurted out, "What's happening?" I replied they would look after me. She shrieked. "They would," I affirmed, calm, slow and deliberate.

'She stopped. A short pause then said, "If you go out tonight, I will change my ticket and fly home tomorrow, alone. Your choice."'

Looking at the tiled floor Maggie said in a trembling voice that she did not go out. I got some more tea and sandwiches for us while she had a little walk.

'Sorry,' I said when she joined me. 'How did you feel?'

'Angry at first, but then I took Mother as she was, still waited for a nice word, a hug—the bad things, well, I shooed them away.' She moved uneasily in her chair and resumed, her voice barely heard, 'At the very least, I escaped my brother's fate. He incorporated her persona, almost entirely. Marriage not lasted, still belligerent and unhappy.'

'Did she ever say sorry?'

'Never. I left soon afterwards. Rare home visits, whistle-stops.'

We sipped our tea in silent companionship. No further need for words.

*

Our first meeting after the seminars hardly differed from the previous ones at the hospital. All the while, the test results were uppermost in my mind. I waited until we were seated before broaching the subject, but to no avail.

'How is your Mother now?' I said in order to close that chapter.

'She is in a home, near me.' Maggie continued, 'Always wanted her own way. She lived her entire life with her authority unchallenged. Of course, now she cannot dictate; she has to learn to accept.'

'A major change for her.'

'Yes. I am mystified as to how effortless it all seems now. I would not have contemplated going against her; she presented a formidable figure to a child. Now I see that it might have been possible, perhaps not even deadly . . . not then . . . so many prohibitions, restrictions, orders, that tied you in complicated knots . . . paralysis . . . In the end, I had my work to hold on to, that was a godsend.'

*

As the weeks passed our meetings became sporadic. Twice, I phoned Maggie, but the conversation was odd. She was out of character. Certainly not the calm and gentle Maggie I knew. How could this be?

'Hello Maggie,' I said.

'Priscilla, you are always upsetting me, 'Maggie replied.

'Maggie, it is I, Daisy, from the hospital . . . '

Now, she started to shout. 'I don't see why you have to keep at me like this. I told you, I do not want to see you at the moment. I simply can't cope.'

'Maggie, for goodness sake. This is Daisy, from the hospital. Can you hear my voice?'

She stopped abruptly. 'Daisy? Of course. Sorry, I thought you were a difficult neighbour. Yes, our coffee meeting, two o'clock?'

At the time, I thought it was bizarre, the illness progressing? Yet, no matter how I looked at the dilemma, I saw a different aspect, the home life that had been so difficult and so destructive.

*

Three weeks later, I came home to find missed calls from a number I did not recognise. I made a cup of tea and retired to my favourite chair. The phone rang again; it was that number.

'Hello?'

'Hello, am I speaking to Daisy Mott?' The voice was not familiar; a young, gentle voice with a sing-song quality to it.

'Yes.'

'May I ask how you know my aunt, Maggie Stuart? That can also be Megan or Meg,' the voice continued and repeated everything a second time.

'Oh, you mean Maggie, Maggie Stuart? Yes, we met at the breast cancer clinic at the hospital.'

I heard a sigh of relief.

'Yes, yes. That is what I wanted to know.'

I must have imagined hearing choking at the end of the line.

The voice went on, 'I am calling to say—' and broke off into loud sobs.

'She is gone.' I said and was now sobbing too.

We recovered after a long while. She continued to give me the details of the funeral, went on to say that Maggie was not in pain and that she was moved from her flat to a home. At the end, her mother and best friend were with her.

'Her mother?' I asked.

'Yes; a coming together after years of being estranged.'

'A healing, before the very end,' I added. 'I'm glad. At last, Maggie was with her loved ones.' Tears were simply running down my cheeks as I thanked her niece and said goodbye.

Sobs again. Images of our coffee after the hospital meetings succeeded one another as I tried to recapture those moments. It was as if we had known each other all our lives. I let out a muffled sob as I remembered the reason for the group, the illness. There it was: time. Maggie had run out of time. All those months she did not breathe a word of it. Why, did she not tell me? Why did I not see?

Maggie wanted friendship without pity.

When we were together, she wished to forget—even if only for a few moments—the dancing shadow of death.

I got up and crossed the room towards the kettle and opened the veranda door to the tiny garden. I arranged my notebooks on the table in the patio among the vibrant reds of the chrysanthemums and the stunning blue of the lavender. I took in a sip of tea, picked up my pen and started to write.

***

Where I'm From

By Sarah Savage

I am from 10p mix-ups from Spar local shops
And drooling over Morton on Top of the Pops
I'm from the rum baba, blancmange and choux ring
And games in the quarry
And sodastream pings.

I'm from watching Madonna gyrate in vest tops
And Sundays with nothing open, not even the shops
I'm from rooms where radios dominated the space
And chairs with their arms all covered in lace.

I'm egg custard and lasagne and bacon and cheese
And Suki the cat wrapping her tail round our knees
And red shiny shoes trying not to get scuffed
And kites on the moors running over the tufts.

I'm from Baked Alaska and Emergency Bunny
And being told I was posh and that I speak funny
Chicken curry with pitta and chips with rock salt
And Fuzzy Felt, Space Lego, Thelwell and malt.

I'm from the North and that decade of dark -
The 70s, the punk, the strikes and the park
Littered in dog shit, graffiti and glue
And paedos and sexists years before the #MeToo.

But Northern I am with the Boddingtons hops
Well after JS Lowrie painted smoke on the tops
And Strangeways and Smiths, the Hacienda and Cream
And living my teens in the Madchester dream.

And now twenty years in that London I've been
Yet I still miss the moors and the rain and the Scene
But I still keep it real with the paths and the grass
As the roll of the years scroll into the past.

***

Ghosts

By Deborah Reeves

I remember the time I took a ring. It was lying next to the sink in a washroom. Finders keepers, I thought. It's what I'd always been told. I was eighteen at the time, at a club with a friend. I showed her and she seemed shocked, which was odd, I thought, as she took dresses from shops and toilet rolls from pub toilets and when she went through the checkout at the supermarket she'd tuck a magazine under her arm to pass through unnoticed; that, I thought, was stealing. I didn't understand.

I wore the ring when my boyfriend took some photos of me. He was assistant to a fashion photographer. You should put your hands on a model card, he'd said, and I'd felt pleased that something about me had worth.

I forgot about the ring, but not long ago I was sorting out, looking for old bits of jewellery to give to my granddaughter and there it was, a deep red stone in a pretty gold setting. I took it out of the box. Slipped it on my finger. Shivered.

This ring has haunted me even though I thought I had forgotten about it. I put it back in the box. Shut the lid tight. There it can stay with my other rings. They all have ghosts.

***

A Cat In The Dark

By Flavie Salaun

Alma was climbing the stairs out of the Tube when she was nudged against the wall by three women coming in the other direction. During the commotion, one of the three tripped. Alma smiled as she watched the other two lifting her back on her feet, giggling.

'Sorry, so sorry,' they couldn't stop laughing.

'It's nothing.' Alma laughed too, and watched them disappearing; their strident voices echoing against the tunnels. They would be having a fun evening out. Letting out a long breath, she tried to ignore the lump in her chest. Her evening in prospect consisted of a work-do before heading back home early. Not what these women were aiming for, or the kind of nights her colleagues usually have, 'where you can't remember anything'. Tonight, she will end up watching TV with Fergal. She took out her phone.

Fancy a drink after work? Soho? Nothing to lose, she thought and headed to the hotel. Fergal's response came back soon after.

Robot Series is at 10 pm. It's live.

The Robot Series. Fergal's favourite programme. She had forgotten about it. When she first met Fergal she had been excited to date a journalist, that was until she discovered that reviewing industrial technology would lead to spending her spare time watching the latest automated machine. She let out a sigh. She'd have to wait for another day.

At the hotel entrance, Alma stood in the round hall with red carpet on the floor, gold chandeliers above and tables dressed in velvet cloths in front of her. Two ladies stood behind the tables; smiles plastered on their faces. She confirmed her name and clipped the badge to her dress. Leaving her coat in the cloakroom, the vivid green of her outfit now appeared out of place. The dress in a 1950s-style retro shop's window had drawn her in and when she first tried it on, she had had to fight with the multiple layers of red underskirts. The shape showed off her waist and puffed out her chest, and she liked that the emerald highlighted the auburn of her pixie-cut hair. Lifting an eyebrow, à la Audrey Hepburn, she had pretended to blow smoke from a cigarette.

The outfit was a little dressy for the occasion, but she couldn't resist wearing it. Straightening her shoulders, she entered the room like Cinderella. The opportunity was there to impress Andrew, her manager. However, unlike in the fairy-tale, no one stopped mid-conversation. There was no music, just monotonous voices mingling against a dark burgundy background. Clearly not a place where there'll be much entertainment, she thought. She reached for her phone.

Maybe if we go by your work, we can have a quick one? I could come by your office?

In the crowd, she recognised the woman from Help Neglected Children. Clearing her throat, she walked towards her when her phone buzzed with a message.

OK. Just the one.

Her smile grew from ear to ear. London, here I come, she

thought. Teeth on display, one hand extended in front of her, she walked towards her target.

'Good evening. Alma Wagner, from Making Life Fair.' The woman turned towards her with a scowl. Not only did she look like a toad, but she seemed to behave like one.

'I am Andrew's new assistant,' Alma carried on.

The woman stared at Alma. There was the classic flinch as she saw Alma's eye but said nothing else. Encouraged, Alma continued 'We're about to launch a new project on malnutrition in schools. We would love to have you on board.'

After a second, the toad replied, 'It all sounds very nice but how would it benefit us? Don't get me wrong, we want to help children, but there are already similar projects in that area.'

'One of our first steps is to create a strong steering group and Andrew would love to have your charity as part of it.' Alma made her face inviting.

She picked a card from her bag and shoved it into the toad's hand before watching her walk away to greet a person on the periphery of the room. Alone, Alma reached for her phone to answer Fergal but instead saw a new message.

Sorry, B is around, might have to stay a bit longer. Should be back for the Series.

'I can't believe it,' Alma murmured, teeth clenched.

B. was Fergal's director. Fergal had long been vying for his attention for a promotion that wasn't coming, and he chose him over her again. Loud voices emerged from a group close to her. She registered one of the men as someone she should approach but stayed still. Her blood was boiling and pretending to be sociable for work was putting her on edge. She fussed with her skirt and took several deep breaths. Waiters passed with various drinks and nibbles on trays. The smell of warm salmon reached her. There must be an adjacent room with a buffet, she thought. No need for hot food though, her skin was already clammy. When the next tray passed, she grabbed a small something or other resembling a quiche, and an orange juice. Swallowing her food, she thought B. wasn't someone she needed to worry about offending.

You could say it's my birthday and you need to leave early? A quick drink and you won't even miss the Series? She wrote.

Deluded Fergal, she thought. Then, she took a gulp of juice and walked towards the noisy group of men. Her poor eyesight and the small print made it tricky to read people's badges. She sipped her drink and squinted at the names until there was no juice left. She was about to introduce herself when a glass was forced upon her.

'Good evening, Miss Wagner. Richard Glasky from Sewed For U.'

'Good evening.' She hesitated, 'Alma Wagner from Making . . . '

'Yes. We've met.'

'Have we?' she replied. Given her bad eye and her lack of attention, this had happened before. Her cheeks warmed up.

'We weren't introduced. I listened to Andrew's speech about child forced labour. A great job you're doing there, Miss Wagner. I think SFU would benefit from working with you.'

'Oh, fantastic! I mean this would be very valuable for us. I am sure Andrew would be interested in you.' Oh dear, she needed to slow down.

'Shall we move? I can't hear you well.'

She was relieved that he didn't react to her burble of words and followed him to the side of the room.

'People are so loud.' He took two glasses from a passing tray. 'It would certainly add to our brand if we could promote that we don't use child labour,' he said from his imposing height. Not that he was very tall; he just happened to be taller than her. Alma's enthusiasm came to a halt. The smell of cold cigarettes coming from him made her nauseous; it reminded her of her mother's grey skin. She examined his beige suit, his pink shirt and the lack of tie. Crossing her arms, she looked him straight in the eye, 'As much as we value a larger network, our charity does not promote brands, Mr Glasky. I am afraid, you've misinterpreted our objectives.'

The way he glared at her; she wasn't sure he heard.

'Your eye,' he said.

She blinked and stepped back.

'It . . . I am sorry. Please call me Rich.' Clearing his throat he added, 'Of course, we don't want to use children's charities to endorse our brands, but we would be proud to claim that we fight slavery to its core.'

Digesting his words, she drank the rest of her glass. Focus on your job, she thought. Get new members. Richard Glasky carried on talking, 'Shall we meet with your team and discuss how we can collaborate?'

'Of course.' She forced a smile and foraged in her bag for a business card.

'If you don't mind, Alma, I would rather take your number.'

It was unusual, but she would come back to Andrew with a new engagement. She dictated her mobile number and watched as his fingers sent her a text.

'So that you can chase me if I haven't got back to you,' he added with a wink, hinting it was some kind of joke. She nodded.

'Do you mind checking that you received it?' he asked.

Her screen flashed with two messages, including one from Fergal.

'Yes, I've got it.' She then opened her other message and sucked in a breath.

'Everything OK?' he asked breaking the silence. She raised

her eyes, forcing a smile.

'Yes, thank you,' she replied and paused, 'My drinks later have been cancelled.' She grabbed a wine glass from the passing tray.

'Alcohol is not the solution you know?' he teased. She raised an eyebrow and studied him. He was of average build; the only thing going for him was his constant smile and his eyes. They were yellow, like the eyes of a cat. A feline, she thought was the right comparison.

'I don't know about you, but I'm done with networking. I am happy to start my Friday evening but won't keep you if you prefer to carry on.' He waited for her to respond. Alma studied the mass of people in their cloud of chatter. Screw Fergal and his promotion. She turned back to Richard Glasky.

'Good idea.' She drained her drink and grabbed more of the quiches from the passing tray. 'Nice venue, they certainly have the budget,' she commented.

'It is, although some of them have other business in mind,' he said gesturing to a couple. A man was whispering to a woman who listened closely, her hand resting on his arm. The evening wasn't lost on everyone, she thought. Irritated, she excused herself and went to freshen up.

'Lovely outfit,' a woman commented, as she passed through the door.

'Thank you,' she replied. 'It is a beautiful dress,' she added to herself and checked her make-up in the mirror. She had applied dark eye shadow, highlighting her nearly translucent iris. It was hard to draw your eyes away if you were to catch hers. They always encouraged further comments because of their colour but mostly because one of her pupils didn't respond to bright light, like black ink in a turquoise lagoon—a condition known as anisocoria. Stroking the satin of her dress, her lips twitched, she would not lose the opportunity of wearing the dress. She applied more lipstick and smacked her lips. On her way back, she spotted Richard Glasky against the wall, scrolling on his phone. She may as well stay with him.

'I thought you might have gone?' she accused him with a grin.

'No,' he replied eying her from top to bottom. 'Your dress is very unusual, and the red underskirts match your hair,' he added.

Frowning, she tilted her head. He looked amused by her silence. The wine diluted her thoughts, but it was a game she could play.

'Thank you. I thought I should make an impression.' She half twirled.

'For your evening out?' he asked.

'For work, and yes, for my evening out.'

'Let me say, it works.'

'Thank you,' she smiled and rested against the wall. She listened to his conversation and let her thoughts drift away.

Later, she was describing how she used to get drunk on cranberry Smirnoff as a teenager, but that now, when watching TV with her boyfriend, she appreciated a glass of cheap wine. 'Therefore, tonight's sparkling wine is a treat,' she said before she saw that she had run out of it.

Richard Glasky put a finger on his mouth and wiggled his eyebrows before he disappeared. On his way back, he was clearly hiding something by the way he walked against the wall. She giggled like a schoolgirl. Opening his jacket, he revealed a whole bottle of fizz.

'What? We can't . . . '

'Here, we are well stocked up now,' he said. 'To the drinks you were meant to have.' They clinked their glasses. 'Tell me about your eye.' He cut through. It sounded like honest curiosity, so this time, she didn't hold back.

'I was born with it.'

'I find it unusual.'

'I suppose it is.'

'Makes you unforgettable,' he added. She flushed.

'My friends used to call me Alma the Witch.'

'It seems you don't choose your friends very well.' He refilled their glasses, slopping the liquid so it dripped to the carpet. He was attempting to dry her hand when loud claps interrupted them. The Chair took the stage and thanked his guests for coming.

'I can't believe it is that late,' said Alma.

'Do you need a lift back home? he asked, but she shook her head.

'Here, keep the bottle,' Richard Glasky said, shifting it into her hand. 'I look forward to seeing you soon,' he said once more. She ignored him. 'At the meeting,' he added.

'Oh yes, of course.' She waved at him and walked away.

By the time Alma went to get her coat, most of the crowd had gone. However, she could sense Richard Glasky's eyes were still on her back as she walked out through reception. Tiny raindrops sparkled under the streetlights, adding glitter to the vibe of central London. She weighed her options. It was late, the night-time shift was changing, drunks were emerging, and people were hurrying to catch the last Tube. One of her arms hugged her waist, to keep the bottle of fizz she had 'borrowed' against her ribs. She turned towards the lively streets and started to walk.

Keeping her head down, Alma almost collided with a staggering couple and then with a lone man. She slowed down. Why was she in such a rush? She passed vintage shops pausing to study the covers of old vinyl disks and posters of France during the Hitchcock era. She caught her reflection. Part of her dress was showing, like an abundance of rainforest and tropical red flowers. She unbuttoned her coat.

Whatever the drizzle, this dress was asking to be seen and appreciated in all its splendour. After all, it had contributed to her evening. Lifting her chin, she put a hand on her waist and the bottle to her lips.

With new spring in her step, she walked down the main road, keeping eye contact with the passing men she encountered and acknowledging women as if they were all part of the same street party. A group of men outside a pub invited her to join them. She chuckled and lifted the bottle as an invitation to toast. She was pleased her eye wouldn't be noticed in the gloomy streetlight. A song from a bar drifted out as the door kept flapping open. Humming it, she headed towards the night bus stop.

Other passengers were already waiting. She observed a couple, his hand resting on top of the band of her jeans, a thumb stroking her skin. Maybe she and Fergal could pick up their evening with something other than the *Robot Series*? Taking her phone out she started texting.

On my way home now. Fancy joining me soon?

The huff of the bus lowering to the pavement interrupted her. Quickly, she sent her message before boarding. On the upper deck, she found a place at the front and flopped down on the seat. The revellers were partying hard outside, she laughed at a drunk girl's stumbling. At least she wasn't that plastered. Her phone tinged. There were messages. One from Fergal and one from another number.

Am sorry, am stuck at work with B. How was the event?

Evening, Alma. It was nice to meet you tonight. I hope we can meet again soon. Let me know which dates work for you and Andrew. Rich

Fergal's reply wasn't a surprise. What did she expect? She hit reply: *It was a good evening. Will let you know later xx*

The last of the alcohol was soothing her body and the dim light made her sleepy. She rested her head on the seat and without thinking sent the same message to Richard Glasky. Then she saw the kisses. Too late.

I had a nice evening too. Hope later won't be too late. Came the message.

She stared at the message as the bus stopped abruptly. The bottle fell from the seat and her phone faceplanted onto the floor. She pushed the bottle further to the side of the bus and swore when she saw the crack on the screen of her phone.

We will contact you soon. Let me agree on a date with Andrew. She wrote back. That should do.

The air in the bus was getting steamy. Outside, the drizzle made little rivers on the windows. Her mind wandered back to what she should be doing on a Friday evening. Maybe she could have a last try.

She texted, *We could still make this evening special at home?*

At home? Came the reply. She puffed.

Of course at home. Are you close to being done?

Sitting straight, she waited.

Yes, I am close.

Then before she replied, another text, *I wish I could be closer.*

A giggle escaped her. She crossed her legs and readjusted her skirt. Smiling, she tapped, *Me too.*

Taking her phone, she positioned it above her and took a selfie of her pouting to acknowledge her deception. She checked her photo and snorted. Below her pout, her cleavage was unmistakably taking most of the available space on the screen. Not the effect she had expected but it could work to her advantage.

My girls feel restrained and are lonely. Would you kiss them better?

Still giggling, she pressed send before she could think further. It was very unlike her, unlike them. Adrenaline was blurring her mind. Her legs jigged.

It was several seconds before the screen lit up. She read,

You're reading my mind. I cannot wait to relieve them.

Her hands flew to her mouth to cover her squirms. With rounded eyes, she glanced at the other passengers behind her, but no one seemed to notice her fidgeting. Fergal was getting into it; he'd never been so fast at replying. A new side of him it seemed, that she had only just discovered.

'New Friday evenings, here we come,' she celebrated, sending a fist in the air.

Her stop was a single red bus post in the middle of some quiet residential roads. She jumped out of the bus. For a few seconds, she stood on the spot, eyes towards the darkness of the sky, the cool night air riffling through her short hair. The alcohol had evaporated, but she was giddy from her text exchange. Her high heels clipped loudly on the pavement and made her hips swing in rhythm. The halos around the streetlights enhanced the steeliness of her surroundings. Her excitement from the bus started to cool down. Let's get home, she thought.

At the corner of the street, she let out a yelp as a screech followed by a hiss sliced through the stillness of the night. With wild eyes, she searched into the darkness. A cat. In the shadows of the trees. A stupid cat in the dark. Shivering, she readjusted her coat around her. She walked on her heart in her mouth. Her ears pricked up. There. In the distance. Footsteps. Leather against the concrete. Subtle, but there. She wasn't going to turn around. It must be another local. Other people did live in these streets, she reasoned. No need to panic. Walking faster, she calculated how far she was from their block. Less than five minutes. At most. One more corner. Fergal might even be home by now. It will be fine. She reached for her phone. Her heart pulsed in her ears. Her hips swung further, and the sole of her feet burnt. Finally. She could see the entrance. She quickened her steps, but so did the others.

That's it. Run. Digging into her bag, she grasped the pass and slammed it against the reader. Phone in the other hand, she pushed the iron gate with all her strength. She knew it would open slowly. Not what she wanted. She squeezed through as soon as she could. A silhouette was coming fast towards her. Her hands reached the bars to close the heavy gate. Too late. There was the definitive *click* of closure, but two hands had already clasped around her wrists. Stunned, she lifted her gaze.

'So, Miss Wagner, I thought I was invited?' That voice. Glaring at him, she couldn't speak.

'I am sorry, I hope I didn't scare you,' Richard Glasky smirked. The breeze was cooling her skin. She allowed her thoughts to adjust.

Her phone screen lit up in her hand making it easy to read the new text, however, the crack at the top masked the identity of the sender.

Alma, so sorry. It's been hectic. Am shattered, but it was worth it. Will be a bit longer. A meeting with Andrew? Think you meant this text for someone else. See you at home. The Robot Series will be on iPlayer. She blanched. He smirked and let go of her hands. Retreating a few steps, she kept studying him in silence.

'Shall we go and have that evening of fun you so looked forward to?' he asked, hands back in his pockets. The silence stretched between them. Finally, she lifted her phone and opened the chat with Fergal.

No rush. She typed and let the phone fall back into her bag.

***

The Garage

By Joe De Souza

The car had to be serviced again and I was a little confused.

I asked my mum, 'Is it a big or small service?'

She said, 'Oh, hold on a minute darling, I'm just clearing the table. That was rather nice, wasn't it, Teddy?'

And my dad replied with suitable graciousness, 'Absolutely delicious, darling. Thank you.'

'Restaurant standard?' But he had already left the room and was analysing the beauty of a perfectly formed spider's web that he'd spotted in the garden.

'Teddy, where are you? OH yes, sorry, Joe—'

'Let them decide, based on your history. Teddyyy?!'

I wondered if I'd get a reduction, or discount due to bad health. I left for the garage with those thoughts in mind. I parked the car and walked up to the manager who was standing behind his desk and a small divider.

He said, 'Hello sir. How can I help you?'

I said, 'I've had fifteen nervous breakdowns.'

He looked away as if in thought and then back to meet my gaze and said, 'Since your last service?'

I was caught off guard but continued in a more matter-of-fact way, 'The car has not been itself recently and neither have I.'

'You've come to the right place,' he said reassuringly.

I looked straight at the coffee machine meaning to make one, and I asked him if he'd like one too.

'I'm afraid it hasn't been itself either.'

'Oh' I responded.

'No, we only got two cups out of it last week.'

Despite this slight setback, I was beginning to feel comfortable and began to tell him about the niggling pain that I had in my knee joint . . .

He interrupted, 'I can check over your spark plugs If you like.'

'Yes, that would be kind,' I said.

I then began to tell him about a lingering old rugby injury down my left leg.

The manager looked bemused, shook his head and then said, 'All right, I'll check the carburettor, but it may take some time.'

'Will it be getting the full service?' I asked, and simultaneously the car began to roll backwards towards me. The manager rushed to fully engage the handbrake but was too late and the rear wheel of my car ranover my foot. I cried out in pain.

*

A day or so later, I was in my hospital bed and was told I had a visitor. It was the manager of the garage.

'How are we today?'

'We?!' I replied, almost shouting.

'I have something for you.' And he opened his bag. I noticed some car tools, and a few nuts and bolts.

He began eyeing up the injury to my foot. He told me he was retiring from garage mechanics and moving into medicine.

'Where are you based?' I gulped.

'Here!' he said.

'What?'

'You've got to start somewhere.' And he reached into his bag and pulled out a large wrench.

***

Waiting for the King

By Karen Ali

Firas fumbled for the neck of his dish dasha and pulled it over his head. The sun was already making its daily arc across the sky and the chill of the morning was giving way to the rising temperature. Soon, the glare and heat of the midday sun would replace the gentle warmth of the early morning. He looked across at his sleeping brothers, lying on thin mattresses on the flat-roofed house, the only way to benefit from the cool night-time breezes. There was Barraq, on his side, arm outstretched like a ship's mast. Should he wake him? No, Barraq was far too grumpy and slow in the morning. Better to get his friend Mohammed.

He had a funny feeling in the pit of his stomach, a bit like a coiled spring ready to leap up with excitement. He hadn't felt like this on any of the other days when he had made the trip. Somehow, today was different. He just knew it. Today would be the tenth day that he made the journey. For six of those, Firas had persuaded Mohammed to come with him. Sometimes bribed with the promise of a bottle of Pepsi from the local shop on their return journey. The disappointment had at first been sharp. Day after day, sitting patiently at the side of the road. The excitement was high at the beginning in anticipation of what they might see, but as the hours wore on, they were still the only ones waiting there. Gradually their mood turned to disappointment and then resignation that yet again they had got it wrong.

'You're going loopy. Perhaps you dreamed the whole thing,' said Mohammed.

'But I heard my father and uncle talking about it. My father said a special visit would honour our town and he would come this month,' said Firas.

'Well, I think we've been here enough times now to realise that it's not going to happen. Don't wake me tomorrow. If you're still crazy enough to think it will happen, you can go on your own.'

Today would be different. He was certain of it and that funny feeling in his tummy was surely a premonition. In his young life nothing as important as this had ever happened and probably not even in his father's long life. His father, though, didn't seem to care. Creeping down the stairs from the roof, he passed through the internal courtyard, being careful not to cause a commotion amongst the menagerie of chickens and goats. He patted the head of Hamdi, his favourite lamb who baa'd sleepily at him. It was a shame that Hamdi would soon disappear with all the other young animals that he had become fond of.

Grabbing his bicycle, he winced as the pedals squealed with age. He would be in big trouble if they found him sneaking out of the house. Last week his father had caught him slipping back across the courtyard after his mission.

'Where have you been at this ungodly hour?'

'Nowhere, Baba, just thought I heard something strange outside.'

'I'll give you something strange. Do you expect me to

believe that nonsense? You've been sneaking off with that friend of yours looking for tourists.'

Looking for tourists was a popular hobby with Firas. He would cycle into the centre of Baghdad, a city where everything happened, unlike the quiet backwater of Kadhimiya, the small town where he lived. There he would look for people who were different, who could be travellers. He hoped they would take up his offer to show them around the city. He never wanted money for this service. It was for the pure joy of listening to their English and learning more about their culture. He thought of the day that he had met Nicholas in the centre of Kadhimiya and had shown him around the ancient town and mosque before inviting him back to his home. Nicholas travelled the world looking for stories to write and Firas and his older brother Barraq, whose English was more advanced, were transfixed listening to his tales. As they sipped hot, sweet tea, Nicholas told them about where he came from—England. He told them how the weather was often chilly and sometimes even snowed; Firas had seen on TV how this strange white stuff settled on the ground and covered the trees and houses. What really struck him was that girls were allowed to play with boys out on the street or even at school. What freedom. One day, he too would live in the West.

'Baba, honestly I haven't been looking for foreigners, I heard a strange noise.'

'Funny how no one else heard it.' With that, his father grabbed him by the neck of his dish dasha and cuffed his ears until they rang.

Firas shivered as he thought about how bruised his ears had been. He certainly didn't want to experience that again. He hiked up his ankle length white robe to stop it getting caught in the bicycle's chain and kicking the pedals into action with his rubbery blue flip-flops, set off through the dusty, winding, ancient streets of Kadhimiya.

'Hi Haider, is today the day?' He shouted in greeting at the small, balding shopkeeper. Haider looked up from stacking watermelons on the grocery table outside the shop and, wiping his hands on the cloth wound around his waist, turned round to smile at the small boy.

'Yes, Firas, I think it is definitely today and he should come by in a couple of hours.'

Picking up speed, Firas wound his way through the awakening souk. The stall-keepers were setting up shop, and he sped past the tables laden with bundles of brightly coloured cloth and breathed in the warm scent of the many spices filling the air.

'Hey, watch where you are going!' An angry stallholder shouted after Firas as he weaved round him so closely that he nearly dropped the tray of baklava supported on his head. On past the mosque where yawning men emerged after their morning prayers. On towards the large, whitewashed villa where he stopped and leaned his bicycle against the outside wall. Gently he pushed open the large iron gate and tip-toed across the courtyard.

'Psst, Mohammed, are you awake?'

'What? Oh it's you, Firas.' Mohammed pulled himself up from his mattress on the floor and wiped the sleep from his eyes.

'I'm sure today's the day.'

Mohammed groaned, 'You said that yesterday, and the day before that and all the other days before.'

'Ah, but shopkeeper Haider said it was definitely today.'

Dragging his reluctant companion by the arm, Firas took him out to his bicycle. They both mounted, Mohammed sitting on the seat and Firas standing up pedalling. They cycled through the rest of Kadhimiya; past small square houses nestled beside tall, elegant villas. Past the river where small boys were jumping in and out of the water and splashing each other amid squeals of laughter; on to the outskirts of town where the houses gave way to scrubland dotted with palm trees and grazing goats. After a few minutes, they stopped and jumped off the bicycle.

'There's the road.' Firas pointed into the distance at the long black line cutting through the scrubland and desert and shimmering like a mirage in the bright sunshine.

'Of course it is. I know it by now. How long are we going to wait before we give up today?' Mohammed asked.

'Come on, let's make sure we get a good spot.' Throwing down the bicycle, Firas led them across the hot sticky road to a flat stone in the scrubland beyond where they could sit and scan the horizon for signs of activity.

'Ugh! It's still wet.' Firas peeled his flip-flops off and looked at the sticky black substance coating the bottom of the rubber.

*

They sat side by side picking up stones and throwing them to see who could reach the furthest. As the morning matured and the sun rose higher in the sky, Firas's initial excitement melted away and he felt a familiar wave of disappointment creep in.

'Looks like you've sent me to find a camel's mother.' Mohammed frowned at Firas, who was avoiding his eye and looking past him.

'I can see someone; I can see a group of people coming this way.' Firas pointed back towards the town.

'It's probably the salt-seller leading his camels,' Mohammed muttered. 'It must be the day he brings in the salt from the desert.'

'No, it's definitely people.'

They both strained their eyes looking into the distance and could just make out the outline of a group of people heading their way. As they got closer, the boys could see that they were from the town, some carrying small children, others carrying flags. Not far behind this group was another group and behind that, another. Soon, there were sizable gatherings along the sides of the road. The boys found themselves having to look between the adults, who stood in front of them, to get a better view. Within an hour crowds on both sides of the road surrounded the boys; the men dressed in their newly laundered ankle-length dish dashas and the women in brightly coloured robes and headscarves or modern Western summer dresses. Young children sat on their parents' shoulders waving the national flag and all eyes stared up the road into the distance, waiting for something to happen.

It started with a low rumble and felt like an approaching storm. Dust whirled up into the air from the surrounding desert, causing the crowd to cough and wipe their eyes, pulling scarves across their noses and mouths. What caused it? Something was coming. A hush descended on the chattering crowd as the distant sound of car engines became discernible.

'He's coming! He's coming!' Firas grabbed Mohammed's arm. 'Let's get a better view.'

They prised their way through the forest of adults until they reached the front of the crowd. With eyes trained towards the sound of the engines, the black specks growing, mutating into a cavalcade of shining black limousines. Firas and Mohammed stared awe-struck as the line of gleaming black cars grew nearer. The only cars they had ever seen were the old rusty, broken-down ones that occasionally drove through the streets of their town. The leading car was open topped and contained soldiers holding machine guns.

'Wow, look at that: real guns,' said Firas.

'Look at the car behind: it's a Mercedes,' said Mohammed

'What's a Mercedes?'

'My brother showed me a picture; it's a special car made in Europe and only royal people are allowed to be driven in it.'

The procession slowed down for the waiting people and standing waving in an open-top limousine was a diminutive young man dressed in a military white tunic ablaze with gold buttons, epaulettes and a collar of red and gold. On his head rested a helmet awash with a plume of long white feathers and his face was clean shaven. Next to him was an older, sterner-looking man dressed in a smart black Western-style suit. Mohammed whispered that it was the King's uncle.

'That's him. It's King Faisal. There he is!'

The boys leapt up and down, waving the palm leaves they had collected on the way, to attract the monarch's attention. A woman dressed in crisp white cotton and a flowing white hijab, stepped out from the crowd and proffered a large basket towards the King's car.

'What is she giving him?' asked Firas.

'Dates and yogurt, of course,' said a young woman standing nearby.

The young King gratefully accepted the offering which he handed to a nearby aide. He waved serenely, scanning the crowd until his eyes met those of the two young boys, jumping up and down in excitement. With a broad grin, the King leaned down, smiled, and waved at the boys with his white-gloved hand, making them glow with pleasure; They'd seen the King, and he'd noticed them.

All too soon, the moment was over. The cavalcade moved on into the distance and gradually disappeared. The crowds peeled off from the road and made their way back to town. Firas and Mohammed, still marvelling at how they had been singled out by the King for special attention, mounted the bicycle. Firas, dragging his thoughts back from the wonderful spectacle he had seen, wondered how he was going to sneak home without his father catching him.

*

A gust of cold air cut through the warm, steamy atmosphere as someone opened the door to the café. The smell of strong Arabic coffee and the fragrant scent of the hubbly-bubbly permeated the atmosphere. The sound of traffic slowly making its way down the Bayswater Road could be heard above the babble of conversation.

'I got such a beating from my father when I got back that day.' Firas picked up his coffee and took a sip, then smiled at Nicholas. It was twenty years later and he and Nicholas were sitting reminiscing about their meeting in Kadhimiya and Firas's childhood.

'I've never forgotten that day; it made such a deep impression in my mind. King Faisal seemed to me such a splendid, cultured man, although at the time I was probably most in awe of his clothes and the car.'

'Did you know that he had been educated in England and was very Westernised?'

'Yes, I realised that when I was older. That's when I made the horrific discovery that he and his whole family had been mercilessly butchered by their own military.' Firas stared down at the table, the mood suddenly sombre. 'Up to that point in my life my love of the West had been based on the Western cartoons and the films I saw and the fantastic cars like the Mercedes, but hearing about that cruel and senseless act was the beginning of me realising what a brutal country we lived in. I knew that I had to escape, to find a better life.'

Nicholas leaned forward conspiratorially, lowering his voice, 'How did you manage to get out of the country?'

Firas looked up at him grinning, 'I got married.'

Nicholas raised his eyebrows, 'You did what?'

'My wife and I decided to honeymoon in England and then forgot to return.' And with a contented sigh Firas took another sip of his coffee.

***

Silence of Olive Trees

By Sinem Erenturk

'Is this ever gonna work or is it already a faraway dream?' was one simple question in Deniz's mind, on her way in the Aegean.

Meanwhile, slowly the bougainvilleas in various shades of vibrant pink vanished from sight again. Deniz pulled away from another small town in her car and left the airport further behind. Soon the shallow, crystal clear waters appeared on the right. The colours changed from light blue to turquoise with the shifting of the breeze closer to the shore. Up ahead, the Aegean Sea seemed perfectly deep blue. The pine trees began as the car drifted away from the coastal road towards her destination.

The warm scent of pine trees mixed with a salty undertone reminded Deniz of times gone by. All these years between then and the first time they had come here. From being two mad love bugs to two strangers. To ease the pain, she opened the window a little, turning towards the breeze on her left. The draught pushed her thin blonde hair out behind her head and her hands untied her tight ponytail. She felt the warm

sunshine stroke her face gently and took a deep, a very deep breath. Later, she would need that.
'Ah, how I've missed that smell. Some things seem to have changed here. There are more houses than five years ago and the beaches pulse with louder music, but . . . ah, the smell is exactly the same,' she thought.

She was jolted back to her journey by Evren's disgruntled voice, 'Come on Deniz, it's 39 degrees. I can't drive without the aircon!'

'Pardon?' she asked as if she hadn't heard.

'It's too hot to open the window,' he continued firmly.

'The air conditioning is still on. I wanted to have some fresh air,' was all Deniz said. She showed no sign of her discomfort at Evren's annoying tone.

Evren carried on, 'Yes, it is on but the whole point of aircon is that you cool the air in the car, not replace it with hot air from outside.'

She ignored his voice and continued to drive quickly along the quiet two-lane road winding up and down beside the thick forest. Local fig- and honey-sellers sat under umbrellas on either side of the road. After a while the stalls were replaced by black and green olives.

Unlike five years ago, neither those rich stalls nor thousands of statue-shaped wild olive trees in the background astonished Deniz. Instead, her blue eyes were fixed on the white lines of the road.

Evren was encouraged by Deniz's calmness. He kept going, saying, 'Why are you always so selfish Deniz? I've been driving here for nearly an hour on a road that I don't know, in a rented car I'm still getting used to. As if the car is not enough, the connection is constantly lost and I can't see the route! Instead of offering help, you open the window in this boiling weather! Can't you remember that it's not all about you?'

Evren's long-cut greying hair, parted on the right, fell down on his narrow forehead, just above his stern green eyes.

'For God's sake Evren! It was you who wanted to come here to see if we could sort out what's going on between us. You can leave me in the nearest town and carry on if you

want . . . But I won't keep putting up with you in this car and I won't let you ruin my holiday with your nonsense and rudeness!' she wanted to say with full force. She wanted to let the edge in her voice build until it cracked. Instead, a dull comment was what came from her. 'Don't worry Evren, we are going the right way, it's only 45 kms to Fethiye. You don't have to check Maps all the time, signs seem enough'

'Ah, of course I can see the signs, too! Am I so dumb that I would check the way online though it's clear? There seems to be a short cut as it shows, I'm trying to go that way!' he said confidently. She should have screamed out of anxiety. She did not.

'Why are you looking for a short cut? Forty-five kilometres is barely more than half an hour, not that long,' was her reluctant response.

'Deniz, stop being so bossy all the time!' Evren yelled again.

In reply, Deniz reached for her phone. After scrolling to Spotify, Björk's melancholic voice came to her rescue. The Icelandic's singer's growling and even shouting sound suited Deniz's current mood. Deniz allowed the song to take her on a journey and accompanied Bjork with her out-of-tune and barely audible voice.

*

After twenty more minutes of driving, she passed the ancient Lycian ruins, somewhat wrecked by soulless present-day buildings, and soon after arrived in front of a stylish and contemporary resort overlooking a secluded bay. She took a quick glance at the resort. Seeing the luxurious, yet clean and simple architecture of the hotel, well-blended with nature with mostly shades of soothing browns and beige was calming. Deniz slammed the door of the car, took her baggage from the back, passed the large and nicely landscaped garden in front of the entrance and stepped into the lobby illuminated by soft and welcoming lights, full of long white and purple orchids.

'Hello, welcome to the Hills Beach Club. How are you today?' said a smart, cheerful desk clerk.

'Thank you. I'm good! This place helps though—it's paradise,' she replied with similar cheer, gazing over the man's shoulder at the welcoming sea below.

'Oh yes! May I have your ID, please? Is this your first time here?' the clerk asked.

'No, but I haven't been here for many years,' Deniz replied wistfully.

'Next time, I'm sure it won't take that long to come back. Just one bag madam? My colleague will show you to your room. It's a beautiful suite.'

'Yes, only one bag.' She smiled back, then glanced around the reception area and down to the sandy beach she could see. The view was heavenly. Evren had vanished from her sight again.

'I can't wait to sink back in a hammock listening to the sound of the waves gently lapping the shore with a cooling cocktail in my hand' she dreamt. Only then did she realise it had been some time since Evren went for a quick visit to the loo. She wavered between messaging him right away or continuing to wait and keeping her cool.

A few minutes later, Evren appeared from behind the statue, exactly where she was staring.

'Where were you, Evren?' she asked tapping her feet.

'I've been driving for nearly three hours so needed to go to the loo honey, is that a crime? What's wrong with you? We are in the best place on earth and you are still complaining, I can't believe it!' Evren snapped.

Deniz's face fell and she felt tiny bugs started to climb her throat inside and outside, she froze for a few seconds.

Evren then offered to help with her little bag, holding his hand out as if he wasn't the one who had told her off a minute ago.

With an unexpected move, Deniz stepped back, keeping her distance from Evren. She was firm, the firmest she had ever been with him. Finally, the words that had been strolling around on her mind since God knows when, flowed out naturally, 'We need to talk Evren.' As the little bugs on her throat were slowly leaving Deniz, she carried on, 'I'll change and go directly to the beach and I want to go alone. Then meet me at the restaurant to talk.'

Evren half nodded without a concurrence. He was about to turn his back to walk on when Deniz called once again determinedly, 'Evren!' and carried on, 'This time come in a clean way, free from all this bullshit. I know you know what I mean . . . Whatever this shit is coming from, I don't care, just get rid of it. Otherwise, don't, don't come at all!'

Feeling the relief in her throat, she walked towards the elevators, without waiting for a response from him. Still there was some sort of numbness throughout her body. 'Was it me who finally said that? With such clarity . . . to him?' She was alone in the elevator.

'Aha, OK do as you like,' he said from behind with his ready opinions.

*

After unpacking her things in her room, Deniz walked down to the golden sands. She wore her hair loose on her shoulders and had a thin, white oversized cotton shirt over a green and gold bikini. Waves were gently lapping the beach in a never-ending cycle. Deniz was on the verge of losing herself in that absolute calmness. The weather inside her head was not so calm though. She selected a hammock, lay down and ordered a Long Island iced tea. It had everything she needed: gin, rum, vodka, tequila and fresh lemon juice. The first three were for finally facing what made her put up with Evren's dark side for years and made her so vulnerable to him. And fresh lemon juice was for standing still and carrying on despite everything.

As she sipped and swung her hammock, one foot catching in the warm sand, the young couple nearby caught her eye. The girl was reading a book while the boy was gently massaging her back and dropping tiny kisses on her neck. When the girl lifted her head, Deniz pretended to be looking at the artwork behind them. It read: 'The people you love become ghosts inside of you and like this you keep them alive.' She slowly turned her gaze away from the couple to the sea with her mind on Evren.

She should have burnt her bridges long before; it had been so clear to everyone who knew them, why not to her then? The romance they'd had on this beach was still a sweet memory along with many other sweet ones. One Christmas he had come back with two large bags containing every treat he could find from the few open shops in the small holiday town they were in at the time. The bags contained everything from her favourite magazines and every sort of cold and flu products to loads of chocolates and sweets and a hot-water bottle in a fluffy red cover scattered with white heart shapes. Those were all to comfort her during her very mild cold. He didn't miss even one opportunity to show her gentle care. And his clever, well-timed jokes about random stuff that always sent her into helpless fits of laughter . . .

'Come on Deniz, don't let those memories take you over. They are in the past, way in the past,' she reminded herself.

Still, she was wondering where this unusual intimate feeling for particularly him came from. Weren't there so many nice men around who were handsome, sweet and thoughtful? What was it in her that found Evren so irresistible and desirable? Was it the same thing in her that couldn't get away from Evren? What was the link between this 'thing' and her endless patience for him? Especially when he'd also become so argumentative and angry with her over almost every little thing . . . Wasn't life short enough without continuously trying to find the missing pieces of a puzzle and fit them together? She ordered another Long Island.

She wasn't after the answers. Even if there were any, it wasn't in her hands to solve them. Still, the questions were important to her. After all, it had taken some five years to be able to ask them of herself. She felt brave. Just at that moment in her life, in her hammock, between the thick forest of statue-shaped, silent olive trees and endlessly exciting sea, her kind of safe place. . .

Then, she heard the waiter's throat-clearing sound intended to make her aware of his presence. He was holding her Long Island on a tiny tray on his hands. She leaned forward to get her drink and nodded to thank him. The hammock slipped unexpectedly and she spilt almost half of her drink on her pure white cotton tunic. Her top was covered in ugly brown and dark yellow in a second. Pure embarrassment ran from the roots of her hair to her toes and she started shifting her weight from side to side.

Evren's voice reached her ears from behind, 'Look what you've done! Can't you be more careful, your head is always up in the air!'

The embarrassment brought the feeling of having to walk on her tiptoes. 'It was my mistake; I should have got up properly instead of leaning forward,' Deniz said with a bitter face.

That was the moment when her friend's question slipped into her head, 'Who made you feel walking on your tiptoes in your past, don't try to find an exact attitude, focus on the similarity of the feeling, then you'll break the repeating chain.'

Evren's grumpy voice turned into her mum's, 'How careless you are to spill the milk all over the floor!' Distress morphed into a grumpiness running through her entire body. By the time she was as if eight years old again, the waiter broke into her thoughts.

'Don't worry madam, I'll bring a new one shortly!'

She turned her face towards the waiter with a blank look, couldn't even find the energy to say a quick 'Yes, please'. She wasn't embarrassed anymore but heavily exhausted. Now, her excuses for spilling the drink had evaporated.

She checked behind her to see whether Evren was still there. She stood up and walked towards where she thought his voice came from. Evren was standing at the corner of her vision, slowly fading . . . And then he wasn't there anymore.

She was finally sure that he had never been there since the split. . .

*

Later, refreshed by a serene dip at the beach, Deniz took the stairs down to the open-air dining room facing the picturesque bay. Her flowy, light blue jersey gown danced gracefully in the breeze and the sun set behind a sea of white boats at anchor in the bay. A modern remix of Lacrimosa drifted from the speakers, accompanied by the sound of cutlery clinking against dishes and the sound of discreet background chatter.

She chose a quiet corner table overlooking the bay through the olive trees. She scrolled the mezzes and seafood on the menu. All delicious, but her mind was still distracted. A smiling young waiter appeared, and out of habit more than choice she ordered vine leaves stuffed with rice and blackcurrants.

She sipped her water and heard a familiar voice, calling her name.

'Deniz? Is that really you?' said a gorgeous woman in her forties with long brown curls.

Deniz rose to greet the woman, who bent to kiss her cheek. 'Begum! Oh my God. What are you doing here?'

'Just some time off work, darling. So happy to see you here! Deniz is my ex-colleague, my love,' Begum said, turning to a handsome man at the table behind her. 'We have worked on so many projects together in the past. Unlike me, she is the hardest-working woman I've ever known. Deniz, this is my husband. We got married last year.'

'Oh congrats, and nice to meet you.' Deniz shook the man's hand in greeting.

'Don't tell me you are in this wonderful place on your own?' Begum asked, inquisitive as ever.

'Actually, yes, I am on my own. You know how it is with work. Good to get away. Reset etc.'

'Well, I'm not surprised darling,' said Begum. 'I hear good things about your company. Tipped for the top I hear.'

'Well, yes, it does seem to be going well,' said Deniz looking down at her feet.

'I'm afraid I need to take this call ladies.' The husband unfurled his long legs from beneath the table and wandered out on to the terrace.

Begum took a large swig from a glass of wine and continued with a lower voice, 'To be honest, I always thought it wouldn't take so long for a beautiful woman like you to find a good match after your split with Evren. All the people in the company were so sure that you two would marry. You were the most romantic couple. We were so shocked at your sudden split.'

'Begum, that was centuries ago. It's all water under the bridge now. Life goes on,' Deniz said with a content smile.

'Well thank heavens you wised up when you did. God knows I never liked Evren, I know he was super handsome, kind and successful but I felt he had a dark side he never showed anyone. I think it was a blessing for you!' Begum extended.

Taking a sip of water from the glass on the table, Deniz smiled, 'Everyone has a dark side Begum, are you aware of yours?' And she meant it. Deniz deeply felt the healing truce she made with Evren. Who would know it would be far more complex than just admitting Evren being a pain?

Begum just nodded her head doubtfully, far away from understanding what she meant, but that was all right.

After a pause, Deniz concluded, 'Look—gorgeous to see you as usual, but I have a sailing course in the morning, and it starts so early. I've never sailed before. It will be an exciting day for me.'

Begum protested but Deniz stood up and began walking away, waving at her. For the first time in many years, she felt as light as a bird finally owning the power to change the narrative built in her for the better, forever.

*

Next morning, she woke as fresh as a flower with sun starting to fill every corner of her bedroom. Golden fingers of sunlight attracted her towards the windowsill for the view. The rising sun shone softly behind the two hills, changing their colour from dark grey to soft greens. Slowly, it made each and every tree in the forest stand out vividly. She poured herself a cup of jasmine tea, savouring it as she watched the new day emerge. She dressed and walked out of the building, without rushing. Bougainvilleas attached to the side of the door welcomed her outside. As she was sauntering through the passageway built out of white, flattened rocks to the beach for the morning's sailing course, a gentle male voice called her name from behind. She turned her head in slow motion with her eyebrows moving up in unison.

'Evren?'

***

Bilk

By Sarah Savage

He adjusted his balls to the left and exhaled a lungful of puff.

'What do you mean you've given the money to your 'effin sister?' he said, the over-loud TV at her end of the conversation tuned to an American sitcom.

'She's family, Sid,' said Achara, swimming in and out of focus. 'You wanna say hi to the little one?'

He focused as the baby slid into view, a shock of on-end black hair; her rosebud mouth clamped firmly round a pacifier.

'I send the money for you, and her, and the restaurant,' he said, stabbing his joint into a Fray Bentos pie foil. 'Not to fund your sister's bleedin' lifestyle. And what the frig is that? I said no dummy!'

'Shush shush shush,' said Achara in a singsong voice as she bounced the baby on her lap, and Sid was not sure whom she was talking to. 'Sister is not here right now, but she sends all her love, like me.'

He slammed the laptop lid down as Achara froze on screen.

'Fuck's sake,' he muttered, hitching up the loose tie-dye pants he always changed into at six.

The light from the open fridge lit a solitary Singha in its spotlight. Sid tapped it expertly open on the counter-top and emptied the bottle into his mouth, which rebelled under such careless handling, dispensing most of its contents onto his chin.

He swiped the beer from his face and neck, and flopped onto the sofa, shoving empty chip cartons out of the way. They slid elegantly to the floor, and a browning blob of ketchup flicked up on his thumb. He smeared it absentmindedly onto the thigh of his trousers and scrolled irritatedly through the Screwfix website, swiping past flexible hosing and into wastes and traps. As he recoiled at the price of a ballcock, WhatsApp lit up with a picture of Achara. She was in a restaurant, surrounded by plates of half-eaten food —eyes red from the flash. He pinched the screen, scrabbling with his meaty fingers to zoom in on what looked like a pile of Mee hokkien with a clearly half-eaten slice of boiled egg lounging guiltily on top of the congealing noodles. Achara, as Sid knew, was allergic to eggs.

He shuffled over to his laptop, lounging crazily against a Plumbers World catalogue, and jabbed a greasy finger at the Zoom icon. But the calling window merely reflected his own puffy face, and a back-to-front poster of Koh Phi Phi blu-tacked to the wall behind him. Achara was very clearly not now available. Sid booted a chip box across the lounge with such force the remaining chips were thrown clear like bodies from a car wreck.

Once he'd lit a new joint, and taken some meditative drags, he returned his rage to the corner. This was a technique he'd honed on the anger management course his GP had insisted on. He'd never worked out why Achara had been there, but Sid was not a man who questioned good fortune, since he had had so little of it. Since she'd returned to Thailand to have their baby, he'd missed her with an ache so severe it could only be muted by copious amounts of internet porn, and an extensive amount of time spent on Zoom. With resignation he accepted that there would be no internet-based relief of any description tonight.

*

The next day Sid was feeling fortified by a full English and a strong tea with one and a half sugars. Even the usual morning rush couldn't dent his mood. He hummed along to Magic FM, easing his van in and out of the columns of traffic. A long night of sweaty dreams in which Achara's fantastic breasts bounced in front of faceless white males had left him resolved in his plan. He'd get over to Phuket before Christmas, spend time with Achara and the baby, see how the restaurant was doing, and check up on the bloody sister. Which meant he'd have to earn about £30k between now and then. He pulled up outside his client's house, relieved to find a parking spot so close, and checked his face in the mirror, scrubbing a flake of egg yolk from his stubble.

Ninety minutes later he was contorting himself round a built-in toilet.

''Effing bastard,' he said to the built-in unit he was fitting. He worked better when he talked to himself, and never listened to the radio lest it distract him from a pesky spigot. He sighed and bent down to cut a hole for the soil stack.

Two hours later he was still making adjustments with the use of a small saw, and sweat slid in sticky streams down the valley in his back. Once all the pipes slotted into place, he stepped back in satisfaction, slurping at the tea the client had brought up to him.

'Now just the cistern to get in, then tomorrow the shower tray, and we're getting there, Sid, we really are.' There was no one listening.

He was pleased that he'd got the unit exactly level—no mean feat in these old houses where the floors were all over the place. His stepdad has insisted on precision in his work too, and Sid had been lucky to learn from the old-school perfectionist. The guy was a violent bastard, true, but he could copper-sweat a tee with the precision of a surgeon. Sure he'd hit Sid a few times, even battered him with a shoe once, but then hadn't he looked after Sid when his Mum had buggered off, and left him a pretty good plumbing business in his will? Sid promised himself a bacon butty as a reward on his way home.

*

Underneath a large orange sign that loudly advertised treatments for 'Fungal Infections', Sid scratched at his groin surreptitiously. He loved almost everything about Thailand, but he did not enjoy browsing creams for jock itch in such a publicly obvious place. Virtually the minute the plane had taxied to the gate at Phuket airport, he'd felt the scratchy blooming of moist-loving fungus on his ballsack, and he knew his familiar, but dreaded, old friend was back. In the terminal, he paid a smirking young woman for the usual cream, which he stuffed hurriedly into the wide pockets of his trousers. He once again ran nervous hands over the bumbag protruding from his belt like a figurehead, mentally counting the hard-earned notes inside.

'Leave it, Sid, you paranoid twat,' he muttered to himself as he set sail across the wide shiny expanse, his slapping flip-flops pushing welcome breezes up the legs of his trousers.

The welcome sight of Mai Khao beach beckoned him from beyond the airport perimeter. But even the palms waving in the late afternoon sun couldn't sooth the unbearable itch of his scrotum. He distracted himself by scrabbling in his breast pocket for a fag, before remembering he couldn't light it until he was well clear of the terminal building. For good measure, he checked his bumbag again lest it had been lifted by a nimble-fingered local.

The crowds in the Arrivals hall clustered like starlings, and Sid struggled to pick out Achara. Eventually a woman in impressively tiny shorts detached herself from the mass of men with their cardboard signs, and advanced upon him, with what seemed to Sid like unnecessary vigour.

'Welcome in Thailand, Sid,' she said.

Sid had taken, even by his standards, ridiculous advantage of the call-bell above his seat, nervous about flying and seeing Achara and the baby again. As a result it took a while for his eyes to slowly focus on the fetching female form in front of him, while his brain reluctantly unglued itself from the insides of his skull.

'Where's Achara?' he coughed, as disappointment swamped his body.

'I am Apinya—Achara's sister. She is busy in the restaurant so she sent me. But she's all ready for you.'

This last was delivered with a wink and small hand gestures that drew a shapely female form in the humid air between them. She then stretched upwards to place a fragrant kiss on his stubbly cheeks. Long shiny hair brushed his arm and he reluctantly engulfed her tiny hand in greeting, handing over a jar of Marmite and a box of Yorkshire Tea Gold Blend in a crumpled Sainsbury's bag.

'English delicacy!' smiled Apinya peering into the bag serenely before leading him outside.

Night had settled, and with it a breeze stirred the palms. Apinya ushered him to a brand-new Toyota Hilux squatted at the kerb. There was an unsmiling man at the wheel, who stared straight ahead while pressing something on the dash with one leather-gloved finger. The boot drew silently open, wafting welcome cold air over Sid, as he threw his rucksack in. As they glided silently down the ramp from Arrivals, Sid dialled Achara's number while petting his bumbag nervously. There was no reply, and Sid caught the gleam of the driver's eyes in the rear-view mirror. He was tempted to slowly indicate his intention to mash the guy later with some suitable hand gesture but remembered that Achara did not like it when he got mad.

*

Business was not even remotely brisk in the restaurant Sid had paid 1,300,000 Thai baht for. It was late, but still.

'Where's all the Germans?' said Sid to Achara.

From the beach out front it looked deserted, shuttered and dark. But when Achara pushed the door open it revealed one table of smartly dressed Thai women who narrowed their eyes at Sid through thick cigarette smoke. One raised a bottle of beer in his direction and gave him a tiny wink. Sid furrowed his brows but still couldn't place her.

'Problem with the fryer,' said Achara leading him towards the bar, as though this explained in any way why the place wasn't buzzing.

'Fryer?' repeated Sid staring down at her. 'What the frick does that have to do with anything?'

'No chips,' said Achara, wagging a finger at him patiently as though to a naughty dog.

'I hope you're not serving bloody chips in my restaurant,' said Sid, leaning over the bar to help himself to an already open bottle of Phuket Beer. He knocked back half in one go and added, 'So where's my little girl then?' gesturing towards the ceiling with his foaming beer.

'She's sleeping, Sid,' said Achara, going behind the bar to fix him another drink.

'I just need to see her,' said Sid. 'I won't wake her.'

When he came back down, the women had gone, although faint laughter drifted to him over the warm sea breeze from the door. He left the bar, squeaking across the still warm sand to where Achara was sitting beneath a tree. He sat down heavily, kicking off his sandals, as she burrowed into him, laying her soft small head on his shoulder.

'How are you doing, doll?' he whispered as he stroked her hand.

'All fine now you're here, Big Bear,' she replied, dancing delicate fingers up his thigh.

*

Later that night he woke to an empty bed. Laughter and the faint pump of Bruce Springsteen drifted to him from the bar downstairs. His bladder ached and he stumbled from the bed, tripping over his trousers which were still clinging to one ankle. It took him a full four minutes to persuade all the pee he'd been bottling to dribble out pathetically. For good measure he smeared some cream round the end of his knob and staggered back towards the bed. He fell across it, kicking off the still-clinging trousers, scrabbling for his phone to text Achara.

He woke six hours later, face down, naked, and phoneless. The sun pierced the gaps in the shutters and the welcome sound of a blender mingled with the aroma of coffee rose towards him.

When he came down, Achara was sitting at the bar reading the Washington Post on a phone, glasses perched on the bridge of her nose. She pushed an orange juice and black coffee towards him and stretched up to light him a cigarette. Her hair brushed his hand and his cock twitched tiredly in his shorts. He grasped her wrist gently and pulled her towards him.

'Hey naughty girl, why've you got my phone?' he said only half mad, imagining her going through his photos, which were sadly only of Achara, the baby, or various bottom-entry fill valves and back-flow preventers in their before and after states.

'I found your phone on the floor, Sid,' she said, pushing against him, so he could feel her hip bones against his thigh. 'You were a bit drunk last night.'

She paused and pulled at his earlobe with her teeth.

'And then I checked your photos, to check you don't have another special lady!'

'Well don't go sneaking in my phone,' he said, putting it in his pocket and making a mental note to change the pin. Then taking pity on her downcast face, he added, 'Listen, I know we've got restaurant business to talk about, but I need a day with my girls—let's take the baby over to Coconut Island and have lunch at that place we like.'

*

The afternoon sun had melted the air to treacle. Sid and Achara lay tangled in bed with the snoring baby between them. Sid was suddenly overwhelmed by a terrifying thought. 'The money! Fuck! The money, Achara!' he whisper-shouted so as to not wake his sleeping girl. He staggered to a table by the window and collapsed back on the bed with the now empty bag, which gaped open like a fairground house of horrors.

'How could I be so fucking stupid?' he whispered hoarsely from behind his big hands. 'It's been twatting stolen. I'm such a bellend. Oh God, Achara, I'm so sorry.' He turned to her with tears in his eyes.

'How could someone climb up here and steal it? Don't be silly, Sid—I put the money in the safe when you were sleeping,' said Achara, giggling and smoothing her hand along the hairs on his arm. 'I found it on the floor with your phone and your ballsack cream.'

'Thank fuck for that!' gasped Sid in relief, mopping his eyes and brow with his pants. 'But I wish you'd told me—I nearly had a frigging heart attack! Let's get to the bank now and pay it in, yeah? It's too risky having it all in the safe here. What if someone does break in?'

'Banks closed at two, Sid. We can go tomorrow, but the safe is very secure don't worry—everyone in Thailand has cash. How else do you think we get a big discount on a new fryer?' Achara said, stroking the knuckles on the fist he was clenching.

'New fryer? Well, yeah, fine, but we need to bank the rest —there's six months of my wages in that safe! And I don't like leaving cash lying around, whatever you say about Thailand.'

He swigged from a bottle of water he found on the floor by the bed and turned towards her, 'Tonight we go to the cash and carry to get a fryer, and tomorrow we go to the bank and deposit the money,' he said with authority.

Achara sighed resignedly, 'OK. But I still wanna have some fun—you've only got three more days before you have to go back!'

'Yes, darling,' said Sid, 'but I've also only got three more months of work in London before I'm here forever. And I still need a business to move to.'

The baby smiled in her sleep as she filled her nappy.

*

Before the plane had even taxied to the stand Sid could smell the damp grass and sock smell that heralded a return to Heathrow. The official bong hadn't even sounded before seat belts were unclipped, but Sid took his time, in no rush to rejoin his London life.

He was one of the last to stagger down the aisle and was greeted with an overcrowded airport bus already pulling away into the darkening air. The Premier Inn on the A4 loomed like a ghost ship over the top of the terminal building, and he shivered and pulled his sarong more tightly round his bulging middle as he descended the slippery steps.

At the Tube barrier, he hooked his phone between his chin and shoulder and dialed Achara for a third time, tapping expectantly on the reader with his card. It beeped, remaining firmly closed. People parted round him as though he were a rock in a river, and passed through the doors in front of him, which opened and shut like a clockwork toy. Annoyance bloomed as he stared murderously at his non-cooperative Bank of Thailand card. He scrambled in his bum-bag and extracted a slightly bent and battered TSB card, which he pressed to the black and yellow reader with frustrated force. The gates opened smartly and Sid shouldered his way through.

It was an early spring evening in London, and rain clouds hung heavy. Sid scratched his arm and recoiled as the top layer of tan came away. His feet, which he'd felt proud of next to Achara's perfectly manicured size threes, now looked ridiculous in their beach shoes—wrinkled, brown and craggy against the cold, grey platform.

He was lucky to get a seat on the Tube, and as he sat down, he consoled himself with the thought of a take-out curry and four-pack later that evening with his mate Tony in front of the Arsenal match. He'd left his crotch-loving fungal friend behind in Thailand too, which was its usual relief, and his mood lifted even further as he remembered he still had a week before he'd have to be back with the self-rimming sinks and gas cocks. And in only three months he'd be back in Thailand, with his wife and daughter for good.

As the train whined away from the platform towards central London, Sid tried Achara's number again. Opposite he could see his own tanned face reflected in the rain-smeared window.

'Hello?' he said with relief as his call was answered.

There was only the noise of windy static, and his own voice echoing back to him.

'Hello, Achara?' he said again. 'It's Sid.'

He jabbed his finger on the screen as the line went dead. The train rattled over some points on its approach to Hatton Cross, and Sid tried Achara's number again.

A woman's recorded voice said calmly in Sid's ear, 'I'm sorry, the number you have dialed has been disconnected.'

Sid felt the pressure change slam as the train plunged into the tunnel.

***

The Beach

By Frank Offer

'It's a gift to be able to create the illusion of light on paper. To achieve that luminosity with a few brush strokes is the work of a true artist.' Will Beckley-Simons was in full flow. He smiled to himself as he moved through the pictures, enjoying the interest shown by the students in the art class.

'In this picture, can you sense the speed?' he asked as the group were mesmerised by Rain, Steam and Speed. 'See how the more heavily painted mass of the thundering engine contrasts with the light brush strokes in the sky.'

'Let's imagine ourselves on the train back in 1844.' He zoomed into the painting revealing figures on the train. 'Can you feel the hot steamy air rushing across your face, the rattling vibrations under your feet and sense the excitement of your fellow passengers?'

'It looks so vivid as if it was painted yesterday,' remarked a middle-aged man. 'How come it hasn't lost the colour over the years?'

Will responded with a knowledgeable account of paints and added an insight that the painting originally included a hare running in front of the train, which is evident in an earlier engraving. 'However,' he explained, 'this is now largely lost in the original as that particular paint has faded over the years.'

The evening ended and all but one of his students left.

As he was closing his laptop, a scent brought long-forgotten memories of romantic nights out with Susan to mind. He turned round, his thoughts taken back to his twenties.

'Thank you, that was fascinating,' said a young lady who he'd noticed in the class earlier.

He smiled but said nothing, feeling awkward in response to the compliment.

'You brought that painting alive for me—I really felt like I was on that train.'

'Th-Thank you,' he stuttered, wondering why he was now struggling to string more than two words together.

'I'd like to know more.'

'Locking-up time,' echoed in from the corridor. A loud jangling of keys reinforced the point.

'I should go now,' he said. He was unsure whether he welcomed the interruption.

'Can you come to the pub?' she asked, twisting her long red hair.

'Er, I should go now.' He edged to the door. 'More next week.'

He wandered out and drifted across the road to the pub, half-hoping she might join him there.

He gazed at the dancing flames in the pub fireplace, his thoughts lost in the past, as he slowly sipped his pint.

*

'You're late,' Susan snapped, brushing her faded red hair to one side. 'Did you remember my new clients were coming round for drinks? I asked you to wind up your class early. Did you forget? I thought it was only Turner for the umpteenth time.'

'Sorry, there was an after-class staff meeting.' He looked away from her gaze, turned his back and made for the drinks cabinet.

'Why do you bother? You could earn twice as much working in the City,' she called after him. 'You could do so much more, particularly now you're not looking after Sophie.'

Pain contorted Will's face. From the moment of her birth, he'd known life would never be the same. As she grew it was clear her life would be limited by her challenges, but she was always so joyful. He was never prepared for it to end so cruelly before she was even an adult. Caring for her had kept them together, but also concealed the yawning gulf that had stealthily grown between them over the years.

He reached for the red wine, but it slipped from his grasp and fell to the floor, spreading a red stain across the new cream carpet.

'What have you done now!' she shouted. 'It's not even a week since that was fitted.'

They argued into the night, repeating the cycle of so many recent nights, eventually heading to their now separate bedrooms.

*

'Do you remember our trips to Brighton when we were at uni?' Will asked. He hoped to focus the conversation on happier times.

'Yes, I'll never forget that seedy hotel,' Susan replied. '"Sea View"—we laughed so much as you tried to get a glimpse of the sea.'

'We could go there again. Re-live old times. Sea air might do us good. Different hotel though…'

'We've moved on. It wouldn't be the same.'

Will hesitated. He knew that expression, but he wanted to give it another try, even it felt like their last hope. He longed to rekindle something of what they had before. 'We need a break. It would give us some space. Just some time away from here. You're so busy now the wedding business has picked up and I'm working most evenings. We hardly see each other.'

'When were you thinking this might be? Most days are hectic.' Susan began walking out the room, signalling the end of the conversation. 'You know I have to prioritise my work.'

'Let's go this weekend—you said the wedding you were organising has been postponed.'

'If we must—but not Sea View, that's for sure.' Susan half-turned in the doorway.

'I'll check now.' Will opened an app he'd been exploring earlier. 'Here's one.' He passed the phone to Susan, drawing her back into the room.

'Looks cheap and cheerful to me,' said Susan. 'Too cheap—probably not cheerful.'

Will scrolled further through the selection, moving up a star and another hundred pounds or so. 'What about this?'

Susan looked at his choice and frowned. She scrolled further up and passed the phone back, 'This one?'

Will gulped at the price, but he wanted the time away together. 'Okay, I'll book it now.'

*

The brewing storm was outweighed by the silence at the breakfast table. Will and Susan each gazed through the mist at the grey sea. The chilly damp air cutting through the gaps in the window frame hinted at approaching rain.

'Shall we walk to the Pavilion and seafront before the rain sets in? It always reminds me of Turner's work here. There's an exhibition on at the Museum,' suggested Will.

'Yes, but I'd like to go to the shops first,' responded Susan.

Will nodded and they set off around the shops.

'Do you prefer this dress or the first one I tried?' asked Susan, several shops into the trip.

Will was lost in thought, gazing out the window at the Pavilion in the distance.

'Will, you're not even looking!'

'Oh, sorry. That one looks lovely. The Jet Black sets off your red hair beautifully.'

'How do you think it compares with the first one?'

'Oh, I prefer this.' Will was struggling to remember the first one.

She looked at him doubtfully. 'I'll get this one, then we can look for a coat.'

Shortly after they left the shop, the first few drops of rain began to fall. It soon became a heavy downpour. They took shelter under Susan's umbrella. Susan smiled as he drew close and he instinctively placed his arm around her. She pulled away sharply.

'Let's go for a coffee there,' said Susan pointing out The Grand on the seafront, which looked as though it may have lived up to its name a hundred years ago.

'Great,' said Will. He was relieved to move into the dry.

As they entered, they were shown to a sea front table with sweeping views of the pier and the coastline. Will imagined paintings of the old chain pier, which had long since been replaced.

'Drink, sir?' the waiter coughed, interrupting his thoughts.

'Oh, Susan, you first.'

'I've ordered,' Susan fired back. 'Are you even here with me?'

'Oh, sorry, my mind was on paintings.'

'Not for the first time . . .'

'Large cappuccino, please.'

'Would you like to look at coats too? I think you've had yours about twenty years.'

'Or we could go to the Pavilion . . . ...for the exhibition. I'd love to see it.'

'Latte and cappuccino,' announced the waiter, presenting Will with a bill on a large silver tray.

Will nodded his appreciation and they sipped their drinks in silence, gazing out to sea. Will pictured how Turner would have depicted the darkening skies and impending storm.

Will was considering different views of the overcast beach, when his eyes fell on the girl from the course and his heart missed a beat. She was sat in a shelter on the promenade sketching the storm. He looked again. Was it her? The windows were rain-streaked and misty. The rain outside was still heavy. And she was partly turned away. But the posture, the coat and the interest in capturing the scene— – it had to be her.

Will pondered what excuse he could come up with so he could go out and see if it was her. He longed to share his thoughts on the perspective Turner would have had on the view. He toyed with saying he wanted some fresh air, or to get a surprise for later but it sounded unconvincing even in his mind.

Will was still pondering when the waiter interrupted, 'Will there be anything more?' It was framed very politely but had an undertone of other people wanting the table. There was a short queue now.

'We should be going,' Susan said. 'Are you coming to the shops?'

Will hesitated. He wanted to be with Susan but . . . was that the girl from the course? There would be time anyway for more shopping tomorrow. 'No, I think I'll wander along to the gallery now. We have our candlelit dinner tonight. I'll meet you back at the room about five.'

Susan shrugged and made for the door. Will paid the bill and made his way across to the seafront shelter, dreaming about what he might say to her.

The shelter was empty except three seagulls pecking at a discarded box of fish and chips and several cans blowing around in the wind. He looked back across to the warm lights of the hotel restaurant to check it was the right shelter and walked to others nearby to be sure, but it was as if she'd never been there.

He turned and made his way to the gallery in the Pavilion, half-thinking she might be there.

*

Darkness was closing in and an evening mist wrapping the seafront buildings as Will headed back after a long day in the gallery. The curators had known few other people spend quite so long there or ask as many searching questions. Will smiled to himself as he reflected on the joy of seeing the paintings in real life and exploring in his mind how they had been created.

He immersed himself in thoughts of the paintings as he strolled back along the promenade. The Cobalt Green of the seaweed and the Deep Green of the sea below blended in the mist with the Burnt Sienna of the rusty pier. And there she appeared on the pier emerging occasionally from the mist as she walked with her art case towards the end.

He picked up pace, hoping to catch up with her, glimpsing her shadowy figure occasionally. He rushed past the amusements, their electronic voices shattering the natural world.

At the end, the wraith-like figure appeared to slip between funfair rides and float down to a level below, which the towering waves crashed across.

'Ah, just like Turner,' he thought as he recollected his talk on him being tied to a mast in the storm to see the colours so he could capture them on canvas.

He raced past the rides and looked down from the barrier to a bench. He pushed through the spray, clambered over the salty railings, dropping towards the crashing waves and mist towards a glimpse of red below....

*

Susan sat in the restaurant as the night closed in. Her emotions swirled between concern for Will and annoyance at his absence without any explanation or apology. She texted him yet again, but with no response. Her annoyance swelled to a deeper fury, overwhelming her concerns, as she fought back the disappointment that he could let her down again. Finally, she retreated to their room with a bottle of wine.

Later, she sent yet another text, before settling down to a restless sleep.

The next morning she phoned the Police.

***

The Waiting Room

By Joe de Souza

I arrived at the hospital and went straight to reception.

I asked, 'Busy?'

And was told, 'There's a steady flow.'

'Good, not long to wait.' I thought.

When I got to the waiting room, seats were scarce. So, I placed myself in-between two men. One appeared to be heavily drugged, the other, who was well built, told me he was a builder. I asked him what he was waiting for and he told me there was nothing wrong with him and he was late for work. He was worried that one of the side effects of the pills was death. Although what he was most upset by was that he had been trapped in a system against his will and all he had done was open the gate for an old lady.

That's when the oddest man joined in. He had bulging eyes and his face was sunken in and he had long lifeless hair drooping below his shoulders. He too found it extraordinary to find himself in this position and began to talk quite eloquently to the builder about their situation.

'Do you realise I've been in this predicament for thirty-three years?'

'You poor sod' replied the builder.

'There was a stage when I was completely medication free.'

'When was that?'

'It was a brief period before I was put on a six-month section.'

The builder went a little quiet.

Then two new patients arrived and suddenly there was an impatience to be seen. One man moved towards the door and was told to get back in the queue.

'I was only looking at the notice board.'

There was a jostling of positions and arguments about who was next.

One man shouted out, 'I've been here since Tuesday.'

Suddenly, the injection room opened. The nurse apologised and asked us for our patience. That's when one of the men who had just walked in, got on his knees and began to pray and so did the woman next to him. During this reciting, they both became aware of each other's tone and clarity; as a result, it soon developed into a competition in general holiness, as they reached out with religious fervour, for the injection room doors to be reopened.

Then it did spring open and the heavily drugged man, who hadn't spoken at all, and the builder rushed to the door together and the previously silent man, said in a loud and clear voice, 'This simply won't do.'

And the builder replied, 'You're all fucking nuts and I need to get out of here.'

There was a scuffle at the entrance to the room and a picture was dislodged, but soon the disturbance was quelled.

When I entered the room, the nurse was on the phone to security. All I could hear was 'Yes, an imitation van Gogh.'

Crisis over, the nurse asked me some basic questions, including how long I had been attending the hospital.

I replied, 'Thirty-four years. Amazing, isn't it?'

She seemed to ignore that and was concentrating on drawing up the jab. She then gave me the slow release, intramuscular injection.

I said, 'Ah, that's better.'

But as she was withdrawing the needle, I let out a small amount of wind. Thankfully, she didn't say anything. As I buttoned myself up and politely said my farewell, I noticed that there was no eye contact and her face had turned into a grimace.

I was just about to leave the waiting area, when I was pleasantly surprised to see the builder and the very quiet man dancing the Waltz together.

***

The Beer Can

By Deborah Reeves

The doorbell rang. It was the builder come to tell me what work he'd done and me to tell him again what he hadn't done. No sooner had I closed the door than the bell went again. A short, stocky, red-faced man was on the doorstep waving a beer can aloft.

'I'm your new neighbour,' he said, then eyeballed the builder, 'and *you* left this fucking beer can on my wall.'

I looked at the builder.

'I didn't,' he said.

'Fucking saw you,' said my neighbour.

I wondered if he thought the builder was my husband.

A young lad appeared at the gate. 'I've come about fresh food delivery.'

I waved him away but he stayed lolling against the gate post.

'Wasn't me,' the builder said.

'I fucking saw you do it,' said my neighbour, chin jutting.

The builder frowned and shuffled and shook his head.

The young lad sniggered.

Chest puffed, fists raised, my new neighbour took a step forward. 'I fucking saw you with me own eyes.'

'It was me,' the builder mumbled. 'Sorry.'

My neighbour jabbed the beer can at him. 'I'm not one to be messed with. I'm telling you.'

'He's apologised now,' chirped the young lad.

'And you can fuck off too,' my neighbour said, turned and flounced back to his house.

'I don't need fresh food delivered,' I told the young lad. 'I've got an allotment.'

He looked confused.

'It's where you grow fruit and vegetables.'

The young lad left and the builder came in.

'It wasn't me,' he said, eyes wide.

He smelled of drink and I knew that he knew that I knew he was lying.

'I want to make something clear,' I said. 'I am not going to give you any more money until you complete all the work.'

He looked desperate and I felt sorry for him, although god knows why, and I gave him twenty quid. Not that I'll ever use him again, I told myself, once this work is finished.

I thought I'd better go and apologise to my new neighbour. Keep the peace. Not that I had anything to apologise for. The beer can was back on his wall, glinting at me. I gave it a shake. It was about half full. I went to pour it away, hesitated, then tipped it up and necked it in one. Dutch courage. I wiped my mouth on the back of my hand and looked up to see my new neighbour's face at the window.

***

Handwash Only

By Trevor Aston

It was just serendipity that I called at that moment. You were at your wit's end, what with the presentation that you weren't prepared for, and then the *error code 27* on the washing machine. Whatever *error code 27* is. You needed to get your clothes washed and dried for going away to the conference. I know you wanted to ask her next door, but I was there so it made sense for me to do them in my machine. And it was me who knew how to get the machine to open its door; hold down the power and the reset button together for more than 7 seconds. You see, I've always said to you, 'Ask me anything Jo, I'll happily do it for you'. I know what a strain it's been since Malcolm left, I've made my feelings plain before. Ok, yes, I made them plain before he left. But you know what it's like when you care about someone, sometimes you can't help yourself.

I'm sorry Jo, I couldn't help myself.

Anyway, it was my pleasure to wash your clothes for you, you've got some lovely things, that bottle green satin blouse is gorgeous. Well, that was a pity, I should have read the label. But I think you've got a real thing about cotton, haven't you, is it the feel of it against your skin? You've always been a very sensual person. Well, you seemed to be, to me. The only thing I'd say is; too much brown. Although I do like the A-line dress with the polka dots, that's fun. No, I was thinking more about the work trousers, they're not cotton, are they? Easy-care is the best for work clothes, I suppose. I still gave them a press, I liked to see the parallel creases running up your legs. Oh, the look on your face when you came to collect them, that was enough for me, you didn't need to say thank you. I had everything in neat piles. Mind you, perhaps you were right about ironing your running clothes, you don't want them to chafe. But, I stand by ironing your pants. Of course it's not necessary, but when you're wearing ironed pants, you have the moral superiority over anyone wearing them creased.

Two weeks is a long time to be without a washing machine though. You'd think they'd keep spare parts in this country, wouldn't you? Who'd think Kraków would hold the answer to *error code 27*. That's why I pay for breakdown cover, they'll fix it in 24 hours, or bring a new machine. It's quite dear, but it's just down to what value you put on your personal hygiene. Now, I know you wash on a Wednesday, so I came round on Tuesday when you were back from the conference. How was it by the way? How was the presentation? Anyway, I didn't want next door nipping in where she isn't needed. I mean, why share laundry secrets if you don't need to? I like to think there are no secrets between us. Then you tried so hard not to let me take your laundry bag, and I know you thought you'd be taking advantage, but honestly Jo, I meant what I said. Take me! What are friends for? I think you know what this one is for. So that night, I put the washer on. It was another load of loveliness! I added double the fabric conditioner out of respect, it imbues everything with such an attractive fragrance. I loved the dress, I haven't seen you in that, quite fitted. Of course, you can pull that off. Not me though. It's not just your running, you were gorgeous before you started. Oh, I remember. I wonder how far I'd have to run before the dress fitted me? I thought it might fit, but it doesn't. It's only the dress I tried on, before I washed it, I hope you don't mind. It smelled of you. There wasn't a full load so I put some of my things in. I liked the thought of our things entwined in the same water, being cleansed together.

I thought I'd bring the clean clothes round to save you a trip. I know it's a bit early, that's why I let myself in. Oh, good news! I remembered to check the washing labels this time. Good job too, I hadn't noticed some of your pants are delicate. So I did them all by hand. Mmm, orchid blossom and fuchsia, and they feel so soft against my face.

Now, I'm sorry, but I think I'll have to move you off the bed to get the sheet; I don't want it to stain. I'll put it in the sink to soak. Before the blood dries.

***

Table 52 Writers

We formed our group following a creative writing course at Richmond and Hillcroft Adult Community College in South West London. Discussions during the course inspired us to continue meeting to read and review our writing. We met at a local cafe, always sitting at table 52, and that was where we came up with the idea of publishing a collection of short stories.

The venue for our meetings has changed, but their purpose remains the same - to keep us writing. We hope our experience will encourage others to take the plunge and start writing.

Thank you for reading this, our second collection of stories.

Sarah Savage

Sarah is originally from Manchester but defected to London over twenty years ago. She works as a teacher and a science and technology writer, but has only recently found the time to enjoy creative writing. Unfortunately she prevaricates heavily behind the pages of other people's books, but has been made accountable for her own creative writing, by joining the supportive community of Table52. She also plays the Alto Sax, which is yet another thing her two teenage boys are embarrassed about.

Flavie Salaun

Born in Paris, Flavie has lived in the UK for over twenty year. A former scientist, she has always enjoyed immersing herself in art, books and travel. It was while caring for her young children that she braved a course on creative writing and met her fellow writers at Table 52. When not walking or running, she spends her time with her fictional characters creating stories. Her next challenge is to finish that novel.

Deborah Reeves

Deborah left home at sixteen. She has had a variety of jobs – waitress, fashion designer, artist's model, teacher. She has lived and worked in Africa, Asia and Europe. Deborah has written stories in her head for many years and recently on paper. She loves being part of Table 52 Writers and all things creative. She was runner up in the Hillcroft Centenary Creative Writing Competition 2020.

Frank Offer

Frank works as a consultant in London to help local authorities improve outcomes for some of the most disadvantaged and vulnerable children and young people, building on over twenty five years of experience. Frank enjoys stories with a transformational twist that bring hope in unexpected ways. This book brings to fruition a long held ambition to be a writer and he encourages all readers who hold such ambitions to take the first step even if the destination is not yet clear...

Celia Gray

Born abroad, Celia has travelled and worked extensively in the US and Europe before making a home in England. After a career in teaching languages, notably French, and caring for family, she has now reverted to her childhood dream of storytelling. An interest that lay dormant for many years.

Sinem Erenturk

Sinem began her career as a young journalist in Turkey's only English newspaper at the time, then moved to pharma where she worked for 15 years. Her life changed dramatically after becoming a mum to twin boys and moving to London with her family. That's when she decided to focus more on her writing. Luckily she wasn't the only one pursuing a half-finished desire. When she's not writing, she's either singing or playing tag with her boys.

Joe de Souza

Jonathan Job de Souza (people call him Joe) had a varied and colourful history, including many years spent in and out of hospital suffering from bi-polar disorder. However, his life turned around with the birth of his son and he hasn't been in hospital since. He calls himself semi-retired from being a sports teacher, youth worker and even an ambulance driver for a Jewish day centre! More recently, he has written a memoir called "No Ordinary Joe" and is thrilled to be part of Table52 Writers.

Trevor Aston

After a long career the media, Trevor Aston has finally applied himself to a life-long interest in creative writing. And none too soon, he's no spring chicken. Now his involvement with the Table 52 group is challenging his belief that no one will ever want to read his stories. You might think differently when you read one.

Karen Ali

After a long career in publishing and marketing, Karen is happy to stop writing about products and instead write about characters, plots and far away places. Motivated by the enthusiasm of her fellow creative writers, she is now attempting to dust off and make some headway with that near-forgotten bottom-drawer novel.

Proceeds from this publication will go to Richmond Borough Mind

www.rbmind.org

The first book by Table 52 Writers is also available from most online platforms

Table 52 - A Collection of Short Stories

***

www.table52writers

Instagram table52writers

Facebook @Table52Writers

Twitter @Table52W

***

Cover illustration by Umit Yanilmaz

Printed in Great Britain
by Amazon

84061383R00068